SOMEONE TO LOVE

JILL SANDERS

GRAYTON

This is a work of fiction. Names, characters, places, and incidents either are the product of the author's imagination or are used fictitiously, and any resemblance to actual persons, living or dead, business establishments, events or locales is entirely coincidental.

SOMEONE TO LOVE

DIGITAL ISBN: 978-1-945100-23-9

PRINT ISBN: 9798672030319

Text copyright © 2021 Grayton Press

Copyeditor: Erica Ellis – inkdeepediting.com

SUMMARY

Head back to Pride, Oregon, to find out what some of your favorite Jill Sanders' characters are up to.

Robin is far too engrossed in running her business to have time for men. She made her living off other people's happy-ever-afters, but that didn't mean she believed in them for herself. But after bumping into the sexy man that had her knees failing, she figured she'd have a good time and enjoy herself. She hadn't planned on the relationship jeopardizing everything she held dear.

George is a love-em-and-leave-em kind of guy. Sure, most of the Jordan men had been, but nowadays, all of his cousins were getting hitched. So when the pretty wedding coordinator caught his eye, he figured he'd enjoy a quick tryst. He hadn't counted on her being the one.

PROLOGUE

Thirteen-year-old George Stevens sat on the beach next to his sister, Lilly, who was playing quietly in the sand with their cousin Riley. He watched his family enjoy a beautiful spring day and wondered what he wanted to be when he grew up.

One of his teachers had given him an assignment that was due first thing in the morning on the subject. He had less than twelve hours to write a paper, but George wasn't worried about the time. He was a straight-A student and did some of his best work late at night. Homework just came easily to him. What worried him was that he had no clue what he wanted to be.

He knew he could pick anything to write about and, whatever he chose, he'd get an A on the paper. His worry went beyond his grades. It was much deeper.

His eyes ran over to where his parents were laughing and holding onto one another as they played in the surf, splashing one another. Just seeing the love that they had, that all of the adults around him had, made him realize one thing.

He wanted someone to look at him like that, someone to love him as much as that.

No matter what his future held, he was bound to find the same thing that everyone in his family had. Even if it took him a lifetime.

CHAPTER ONE

Robin had heard the story of how her parents had fallen in love more than a hundred times. Why then did it seem almost impossible for her to find the same kind of love that they had?

Robin's first boyfriend, Drew, had ended up being a jerk-face cheater. Of course, she had not expected to find the love of her life at fifteen.

Her next boyfriend had broken things off with her less than a month after their first date.

She went through four more boyfriends before graduating high school and two more in college before she'd met Chris.

So then, watching what she believed was the man of her dreams walk away from her holding another woman's hand had completely broken her heart.

Carly, the other woman, was a cheerleader and almost ten pounds skinnier than Robin. That in and of itself wouldn't have been a big deal if the girl didn't have a very impressive pair of D-sized breasts, whereas Robin was stuck with her stupid B cups.

She'd given the man a year of her life. She'd done everything to ensure that Chris had been completely happy the entire time they'd been together. She'd attended every college party or game that he'd wanted to go to. She'd even sat by him, completely bored, most Friday nights when he'd sat on the sofa playing games while other couples went out and had fun.

How a full grown twenty-three-year-old man could choose to spend most of his time glued to video games instead of spending it with his girlfriend was beyond her.

But, seeing Carly, one of the college's most popular cheerleaders, walk off with her man had set Robin's back teeth to grinding.

Carly had been out for blood since the moment Robin had rejected being her partner for an English project earlier that year.

Robin's 4.0 grade point average would've taken a dive if she'd partnered with the bleached blonde who quite literally didn't get why the book was called *The Color Purple* when it had nothing to do with fashion or the singer Prince.

That had just been the first of the woman's offensively stupid remarks in class. As the school year progressed, her statements grew bolder and, if Robin could believe it, more calculated. It was almost as if she was disrupting class and saying stupid things on purpose.

Robin was too busy and too focused to spend a moment worrying about the woman messing up her grades, which is why, she believed, Carly changed gears and set her sights on Chris.

Even though Chris could be childish at times, he was still one of the most popular men on campus, mainly because everyone knew the family he came from. The wealth. The power and everything else Chris's money could afford.

When she'd first met Chris, she'd had no idea who he or his family was. Which is why, at least in her mind, Chris had initially shown an interest in her.

After she'd found out about him, she'd tried to convince herself that it didn't matter. If anything, it was one reason she didn't want to continue dating him.

She'd known too many people over the years who used their position to get what they wanted.

Chris hadn't been like that. Well, not at first, anyway.

Robin had been so devoted to the man, she hadn't seen anything like Carly coming. In her mind, Chris had been the one. Sure, there was the annoyance of his gaming and his absolute love of sports.

Not that Robin didn't appreciate a good football game every now and then, but Chris had been the kind to strip down to boxer shorts and paint his entire body green and yellow.

Do you know what it does to a woman to be seen having dinner in a restaurant after a game with a man like that? Everyone they bumped into looked at her funny. They had almost all the time anyway, since she'd felt so out of place everywhere that he'd taken her.

It was as if there was a sign on her forehead saying, yes, I'm from the other side of the tracks. She'd been accused of dating him for his money so often that she had started questioning why she was still with him.

Getting over Chris hadn't turned out to be that hard, after all. It helped that he'd dumped her only a few weeks before she'd graduated.

Then her sister had come up with a crazy idea to start their own wedding business. Robin had spent an entire week crunching numbers to see if the idea was sound.

She'd been happily surprised when, according to her calculations, the business would be a good investment for their inheritance. Less than a month after graduating, she and Kara had packed up and moved to Pride, Oregon, the small town where they had spent most of their childhood vacations.

The town where their parents had been snowed in one Christmas and ended up falling in love.

One of Robin's favorite places on earth.

For the first year, Sunset Weddings did what she'd projected it would do. It grew. Made them enough money that she no longer had to fear.

Then Kara had started dating Conner Jordan.

Robin had been really happy for her sister. Honest. She liked Conner. Actually, she liked all the Jordans.

There were so many of them and sometimes she'd had a difficult time keeping track of who was who. Especially during the last big wedding they'd held for Suzie Jordan and Aiden Brogan.

Apparently, that's when Kara and Conner had bumped into one another and had started dating. Shortly after, her sister moved into the apartment above the local grocery store with Conner.

That had left Robin alone in the small two-bedroom cottage they had purchased along with the massive barn that hosted their venue, which sat directly along the beach.

Robin didn't mind living alone in the small place. She quickly turned the other bedroom into an office, since she needed the space to work.

But then Kara had been shot and it appeared that there was a land developer out to not only harm them but somehow take their land away.

She'd never been more afraid for her sister and her life before. She'd never imagined anything like this would happen in a small town.

Seeing Kara lying in the hospital bed, her left arm tucked close to her body, Robin had been so concerned for her little sister that she'd started questioning her choice to come to Pride in the first place. She grew angrier towards the man who had dared to harm Kara.

It was going to be a long road to recovery for her sister, but she could tell that Kara was completely happy and, shortly the incident, she'd become officially engaged to Conner.

Robin was happy for them. Really.

Now that their parents had retired and moved to Pride, and with her sister getting married soon, she tried to be as happy as she could. Her family was coming closer together and growing bigger.

Her parents had always talked about moving to Pride after her father's retirement, when they no longer had to live in the city for jobs. She was excited that they had decided to build a new home in Hidden Cove, a new housing subdivision that the Jordan family owned, which sat just outside of Pride.

Conner and Kara were having a home built just down the street from her parents' new place.

With Kara injured, Robin was left to run the business herself. They had more than half a dozen employees that helped them out during each event, but that left the everyday tasks that her sister usually handled to her.

Which meant that every moment of her time was consumed by work. So, when it was decided, without her input, that she needed a bodyguard of sorts, she didn't put up much of an argument. After all, what did she care if there was someone walking around the grounds all the time looking out for the madman who had shot her sister?

She'd seen George around town plenty of times. What she'd never done is actually talked to him. So when he'd shown up one morning, claiming that he was there for her protection, she'd waved him away. She'd been too busy to care.

George wasn't really a Jordan. Well, he was, but his last name was Stevens. His mother, Lacey Jordan-Stevens, was the mayor of Pride and his father, Aaron Stevens, was the town's doctor.

She knew that George had an older sister, Lilly, who owned her own boutique, Classy and Sassy, in town. Lilly owned the successful business with her cousin Riley. The two women had married the twins who owned the local pizzeria, Baked.

The rest of the Jordan clan, as everyone in town called the family, was just as successful. Successful, but also known for being extremely hardworking.

The Jordan family owned one of the town's local restaurants, the Golden Oar. It was considered one of the best places to eat along the Oregon coast.

They also owned Jordan Shipping, a shipping company that was known globally, along with a bed and breakfast along the shoreline that had some of the cutest cabins. A lot of her own guests stayed there during bigger events.

So when Todd Jordan contacted her and mentioned he'd like to hire and pay for security, she'd agreed. She had to admit that she didn't know exactly what George did for a living. For the first few days, he stayed out of her way, and she barely knew he was there. She had seen him walking around the building during her scheduled events and, afterwards, he even helped her clean up.

The most she knew about George Stevens was that each time she'd seen him over the past year that she'd lived in Pride, he'd had a different woman on his arm.

She knew the type. A player wasn't hard to spot. After all, he had the standard rugged good looks of all the Jordan men.

He was tall. Though not as tall as his cousins, he was still over six foot. At five foot seven herself, she was always looking up to him.

He had sandy brown hair, although his was a deal straighter than most of the other Jordan men.

He also had different eyes than the other members of his family. Those haunting silver eyes sometimes drew her in and locked her there until she forced herself to blink and look away.

The fact that she spent most of her time around him

thinking of how different he was from his cousins worried her.

George was a player. She'd known it the moment she'd met him earlier last year. She kept trying to warn herself of that fact, hoping it would make him less appealing to her. It didn't.

She'd first found herself watching him at his sister's wedding last year, which had been the first wedding that she and Kara had organized in Pride. Their venue, the old red barn they were now in, hadn't been quite finished with its reconstruction, so they'd held the wedding up at the new couple's house. The place had been gorgeous. It overlooked the town of Pride and was certainly big enough for the outdoor event.

If she was honest with herself, George was the first man she'd noticed. The attraction to him had been instant. So had the annoyance when she'd realized he was a player.

She had even doubted at one point that he knew the name of his date for the evening. She noticed that he had kept calling her babe and when he went to introduce her to someone else, he just called her his date.

The extremely good-looking woman had giggled and introduced herself as Jennifer. Each time she'd introduced herself to someone in his family, he had looked bored or preoccupied.

The following weekend, she'd seen George with another supermodel type at his family's restaurant. The fact that the woman had almost been sitting in his lap assured Robin that he'd moved on.

Each time she'd seen him over the year, he'd had

another woman on his arm. She was beginning to wonder where he met all of them. After all, Pride wasn't that big of a town.

Now, however, she'd been in town for over a year and had yet to go out on one date.

The longer George stuck around her place of business, the more she wondered what his uncle had to do to compensate him for giving up his carefree life.

For the first few days, George had focused on making rounds outside the building and helping her clean up.

When they found the man who had shot her sister at the bottom of a cliff off the coast of California, she was surprised that George continued to stick around. Since most of her events happened on the weekends, she had only seen George a few days each week.

Wedding rehearsals and dinners usually happened on Friday nights, followed by the main event of the wedding, which consumed all of her Saturdays.

Most Sunday mornings there was a church group, followed by whatever other event was scheduled for the day. Sometimes it was a birthday or anniversary party, or a baby shower.

A month after getting shot, Kara was able to lend a hand with organization, but so far, Robin hadn't let her sister lift an actual finger around the place. Not when she still struggled to hold anything in her left arm.

Since their mother was a physical therapist, Robin knew that it was only a matter of time before her sister would be back up to speed.

It had been five weeks since her sister's shooting, and this weekend's party was a dual gender reveal party for cousins Lilly and Riley, who were pregnant at the same time by twin husbands Corey and Carter. The brothers owned the local pizzeria in town called Baked.

That meant that George would be a guest instead of a security guard. She wondered instantly what kind of woman he'd have on his arm for this event. Something close to jealousy crept in, and she was in a bad mood before the event. Hoping no one would notice, she went about her business and tried to not keep an eye out for the man she'd had a major crush on for the past year.

CHAPTER TWO

George stood back and listened to his mother talking quietly to his sister, Lilly. How had he allowed his family to talk him into coming to a stupid baby party in the first place.

The rest of his cousins had been roped into attending as well, which meant he wasn't the only man sitting among a bunch of pink and blue balloons and other baby decorations.

He really was excited to find out what gender both his sister Lilly's and his cousin Riley's babies would be. His entire family was excited to find out.

Especially his mother. Lacey Jordan was, according to many, the head of the Jordan clan, even though her brother Todd was the oldest. Everyone in the family knew it was actually Lacey that ran the family.

She was not only the mayor of Pride but the mayor of the family, a role his mother had taken to heart his entire life.

She might be the smallest of the family, but she was, at least in his mind, the strongest.

So when she'd informed him that he needed to start playing security for Sunset Weddings after Kara had been shot, he'd dropped everything he had going, including his position as a junior lawyer at a small law firm in Portland, where he'd worked since finishing law school in California.

He had worked so hard to finish the degree the past few years that when he'd finally graduated, he hadn't known what to do with himself. So he'd taken the first job he'd been offered. The lower position at the firm allowed him enough personal time to play just as hard as he'd worked over the previous few years. He knew he had been overdoing it a little and supposed he was making up for all the lost time during his studies when he'd neglected to have a life.

Playing babysitter for the wedding sisters, as he had been referring to them since he'd first met them at Lilly's wedding, had not been on his agenda. But when his mother had called and insisted, he'd cleared his schedule for the weekends and moved back home so he could babysit.

Then again, watching the pretty brunette rush around the massive barn for work hadn't been that much of a chore. He'd never seen anyone work as hard as Robin Jenkins.

He knew that her parents had been longtime friends of his family and could remember seeing the sisters several times when they were younger. They had occasionally visited Pride during the holidays or during the summers, staying at this aunt's bed and breakfast. There were several families that often visited, such as Ric, Rob, and Rose Derby, who visited Pride almost every summer and were like family.

When they were younger, the two sisters were hard to tell apart. Now, however, he could tell the difference between them even if he was blindfolded. It was strange, he'd never thought of them as pretty before. Well, pretty, but not worth a second thought. Not when he'd had a line of women after him, especially after he'd started taking law classes in college.

It had been as if he was wearing a badge on his forehead that said *someday I'll be a lawyer*. The moment he started school, women had flocked to get his attention. Now that he'd graduated, that number had easily doubled.

Of course, when he'd been living on campus and attending all the right parties, he'd had his pick of college women. After school, he'd rented a small townhouse near the firm he worked at in Portland, and things had changed slightly. He'd ended up hitting a few bars each weekend with friends instead.

Now, however, having been stuck helping Robin out for the past few weeks, he was having a difficult time not noticing how extremely attractive she was in his sex-starved state. Watching Robin bustle around the old barn had him not only entertained but also extremely turned on.

The way he figured it, he could either try and convince Robin to have a little fun for the remainder of his time in town or he'd need to do something to get his mind off sex.

How long had it been since he'd been with someone? A few weeks before his mother had called and said that his uncle had asked him to come back into town for a job.

The fact that he'd been the first one Todd had thought of had honored him. Until he'd found out what the job was. Of course, his uncle being smart, he hadn't mentioned what he'd be doing until he'd agreed and come back to Pride. Then it had taken a meeting from his mother to convince him further.

It wasn't as if George didn't have the time off from work. Actually, he'd been thinking of quitting the job and looking for something more challenging and closer to home.

At this point, he was just happy to be back home during the holidays.

It was a week after New Year's, which meant that he had been in town for almost three months. He was growing restless and extremely horny. Hell, he hadn't even had anyone to kiss at the New Year's party.

Instead, he'd stood by and watched as every one of his cousins around him had enjoyed the party with someone. Even his sister was wrapped in her husband Corey's arms.

After a moment, he'd realized that he was the last single Jordan standing. Every one of his cousins was either married or otherwise intertwined. Or, in the case of his cousin Jacob, entangled. After all, Jacob and Rose had been flirting around each other for as long as anyone could remember.

Currently, everyone in town believed that the couple were actually living together and, since the New Year's party, it had become pretty obvious they were a couple.

Which left George in a class all by himself. Single.

In the past, he wouldn't have cared, but since he'd turned twenty-five, he'd found himself thinking about his future more.

He only had a few months before he'd need to start looking for another job or go back to work in Portland. What his uncle was paying him covered most of his bills, but still, he couldn't continue to babysit and expect to keep his career afloat.

It was funny, when he'd decided on a law career, he'd always dreamed of returning to Pride and opening up his own firm. He'd dreamed of going to the local courthouse and fighting to protect the innocent, but the closer he'd gotten to the goal, the more he'd realized that his career would most likely take him away from his home.

Facts were facts. Pride just wasn't big enough to support a lawyer.

It was one of his greatest downfalls, the inability to jump at something he wanted and sacrifice everything to get it. It wasn't as if he was a chicken, just... cautious.

Then he realized that being stuck in Pride the last few months hadn't been such a burden. Especially with the nice distraction of being around Robin on a regular basis.

His eyes scanned the crowded party for Robin, and he smiled when he noticed her in the corner, helping refill a few guests' drinks.

She'd worn her long dark wavy hair down for the

party. Today's outfit consisted of a cream-colored top with black dress pants and sensible heeled boots.

He always looked forward to the fancier parties when she wore a dress so he could get a look at those sexy legs of hers. They were the sexiest legs he'd ever had the pleasure of looking at. He wondered if they were as smooth as they looked, which got him wondering about the rest of her.

"You aren't paying attention." His sister stabbed him in the ribs with her finger.

"Ouch." He winced, then wrapped his arm around Lilly's shoulder. In the past few weeks,' he'd noticed her baby bump growing bigger. "What?"

His sister smiled up at him. "We want you to video." She motioned to his phone on the table. "When we release the balloons."

"Why me?"

"You have the steadiest hands," his mother joked.

"Besides, you've been hanging around for a few weeks now. You've got to know all the ins and outs of this place."

He shrugged as his eyes moved back to where Robin had been. Yeah, he knew all the ins and outs of this place. It wasn't a difficult business to follow. People paid the sisters a lot of money to organize and host parties. There were flowers, desserts, food, and decorations.

It seemed simple enough to him.

Lilly nudged him again. "You know, for the best location and angle to video from. We're going to be standing in the center. Just there." His sister pointed to the middle of the dance floor. "Each couple will pull one of those strings." She motioned to the two white strings that had been tied to the banister on the second-floor balcony. "When we pull those, the balloons will come down and fill the dance floor, so you'll want to be somewhere you can see all four of our expressions clearly as well as get the balloons and the crowd's reaction."

Grabbing his phone, he stood up. "I'll walk around and see where the best location is."

"You have half an hour before the reveal," Lilly warned.

"I'll be ready," he promised and started walking towards the dance floor. He'd had every intention of finding the best place to record from, but then he spotted Robin heading up to the balcony and, without thinking, he followed her up the stairs.

All of the guests were down on the main level of the barn where more than a dozen large circular tables had been rolled into position, covered with pink and blue tablecloths and filled with decorations. Long tables sat along the side of the room, holding all of the food and drinks for the guests. Two massive tables with plaques marked with each couple's names were piled high with gifts.

He had just come up behind Robin when she suddenly turned and bumped solidly into his chest.

"Oh!" She gasped as his arms wrapped around her to keep her from toppling over. When she recognized it was him, she pasted on one of her hostess smiles he'd seen so many times before.

He'd seen it every time she'd worked a party or event. He'd been wondering what her real smile looked like.

The one she used when she was truly enjoying some-thing. That made think about what she looked like laughing or even what her laughter sounded like. He'd heard her giggle politely several times in the past, but he had yet to hear her real laugh.

His eyes ran over her flawless skin, her soft brown eyes, her perfect mouth. She had the kind of lips that begged to be kissed.

"Did you need something?" she asked, getting his attention. Her eyes bored into his and, for a moment, he completely lost his train of thought.

She slowly crossed her arms over her chest and tilted her head at him as if she were waiting for him to talk.

"Videos." He pulled out his phone from his pocket. "My sister put me in charge of finding the best spot to record from."

Her smile slipped slightly when his eyes moved down to her lips again. It was as if a magnet kept pulling his eyes down there and his mind kept thinking about what it would be like to taste them.

"The best place to video from is just..." She placed her hands on his shoulders and, for a moment, he noticed something change in her eyes. Then, before he could figure out what it was, she nudged him forward until he stood looking over the balcony. "Here. You can see every-thing from right here. You'll get the best shot of the balloons dropping and of the crowd below."

When he noticed that her hands were still on his shoulders, he smiled and glanced down at them. She stepped back and dropped her hands with a slightly shocked look on her face.

"I..." She glanced around and, before she could move away, he took her elbow.

"Robin." He didn't know what had caused him to reach out to her, but he didn't want her to go just yet. He frantically searched for something to say that would keep her there with him. Something smart. Something witty that would make her laugh. "How do you know which rope goes to who?" Not that, he thought.

She glanced down at the two ropes in her hands, the ones she'd come up here to untie and take down to the waiting soon-to-be parents so they could pull them and release the colored balloons.

When a genuine smile crossed her face, he lost his breath.

"I have my ways," she said with a slight chuckle.

He moved a little closer to her. "So, you already know what they're having?"

She laughed again. "Dr. Stevens was instructed to tell only me. I ordered the balloons and have arranged everything."

He glanced over to the two massive black bags, which he assumed held the balloons that would reveal what gender both his sister's and cousin's babies would be.

"How did you get those up there?" he asked, suddenly worried as a flash of Robin standing on a ladder all by herself as she arranged the display flooded his mind.

She shook her head as a slight frown played on her lips. "I... used a pully." She motioned to the ropes. "These will release the pully. I normally use them to put streamers up."

He remembered seeing streamers hanging from the ceiling during several of the recent parties but had never asked her how she'd accomplished the feat before.

This time, Robin glanced down at his hand, which was still holding her arm gently. Instead of letting it go, he took a step closer to her.

"I... My uncle has said that he thinks you'll be safe enough for me to return to school by the end of the month." He didn't know why he was telling her this, but he figured she had a right to know.

He watched an array of emotions cross her eyes before she gathered herself and gave him a brisk nod.

"I can't thank you enough for all your help over the past few weeks," she said.

"I was thinking"—he moved a little closer—"that with our remaining time, we could entertain ourselves a little." His hand moved up her arm until he was cupping her face. He heard her breath catch a moment before he bent down and placed his mouth over those lips he'd been dreaming about.

CHAPTER THREE

What was going on? Robin tensed for a moment before her body completely took over as George's lips brushed against hers.

How long had she dreamed of this? Since the first day he'd shown up to protect her and her business.

She had chalked it up to going so long without getting a man's attention and, suddenly, there had been a good-looking man watching her every move.

She knew what he was and there was no way she was going to waste her time trying to gain a little of his attention. She had far too much work to do.

That thought seemed to jolt her back to reality. She was standing within eyesight of everyone in his family plus half of the town of Pride, kissing George.

She jerked back quickly, almost losing hold of the two ropes she'd come up there to get in the first place.

"I... need to..." She turned and left without so much as another word to him.

For the next hour, she stood by and watched the

happy couples celebrate the coming births of their new babies.

Lilly and Corey were expecting a boy, and Riley and Carter a girl. Both families seemed completely thrilled at the news.

Robin wondered what gender her eventual child would be. Of course, most people hoped for one of each. She supposed she would be happy with either.

Then again, the first step would be to go on an actual date once in a while. Which had her thinking about George's kiss. What had he meant by it? Was he toying with her?

She'd seen the type of woman he usually had hanging off his arm. Most of them were blonde and busty with empty personalities.

There was no way he was actually interested in her. Was there?

That question loomed over her for the remainder of the party. She avoided him or tried to, at any rate. After all, if he'd packed that much of a punch with just a little kiss, what would happen if she was left alone with him?

"What do you think you are doing?" she asked as she walked into the kitchen shortly before the party wound down.

Kara was standing just inside the kitchen, standing on a stepladder and trying to lift down a large platter from a cupboard.

Her sister's left arm was still in a sling, tucked close to her side.

Kara almost toppled over on the short ladder she'd been standing on.

"Don't do that," Kara hissed. She glanced towards the door. "You scared me. I thought you were...."

Robin leaned against the door and smiled. "Conner?"

Kara smiled and rolled her eyes. "He won't let me lift a finger."

"This"—she motioned slowly to her sister standing on the ladder and trying to lift a heavy platter down— "is not what I would deem just lifting a finger."

"No," Kara said, shaking her head and stepping down from the step. "I suppose not. I thought it was lighter than that." She motioned to the platter. "Would you?"

Robin walked over, stepped up on the ladder, and took the platter down. "What do you need this for?"

"I'm going to make a special surprise for Conner this weekend." Kara took the heavy thing from her and tucked it under her good arm.

For what it was worth, Robin could tell how happy her sister was with Conner. She was truly excited about planning her sister's wedding.

With her parents living in town, she knew that the wedding plans were going to go smoothly. Her mother, after all, was where the sisters had gotten their love of planning elaborate events in the first place.

"Please, don't tell Conner I was up on the ladder," Kara asked with a smile. "I told him I wouldn't take chances with my arm." She waited for Robin to nod in agreement before stepping out of the room.

Most of the kitchen crew had already gone home for the evening, which left Robin to clean up. In the past, before Kara had been shot, it had been the two of them.

Now Kara was back part time, but just doing basic

things like making phone calls to place orders and helping with receiving and deliveries. It was down to just her cleaning up. Not that it was a difficult task, but working alone meant that it would take twice the time.

On occasion, George had helped out.

She'd temporarily hired Emma Auston to help out, but she'd been out of town this weekend.

She could hear that the party had died down out front since there was no more noise coming from the barn. The kitchen crew had left the back room spotless, which meant that her only remaining task was out front.

Stepping out into the main part of the barn, she took a moment to take a breath, enjoying the sweet smells of candle wax, cake, punch, and happiness.

"Everyone's left," someone said, and she spun around and almost squealed with surprise. "Sorry," George said, walking down from the stairs. "I didn't mean to startle you."

"You didn't," she lied. She tried to recover quickly. Her heart was racing, and she knew it had nothing to do with being caught off guard.

He stopped at the base of the stairs and looked around.

"My family cleaned up before they left." He motioned around.

Sure enough, the entire place was cleaned of all trash and party mess. The only thing left for her to do was stack the chairs against the walls. Even that, she figured, could be done in the morning after she'd gotten some rest.

"They're some of the best party guests," she said with a smile as she felt her heart jump in her chest. It was strange—over the past few weeks, she'd felt the same each time he'd been around. But now, her heart was beating twice as fast and her palms were growing damp.

"Do you need any help putting the chairs away?" he asked her.

"No, I'll leave them for tonight. After all, I'll just have to bring them down in the morning again. They can stay put for now." She leaned against the post of the stairs and glanced around. "It was a fun party."

He smiled. "A boy and a girl will be joining the family in a few months." He sighed as he looked out over the empty barn. "It was the best party of the year," he agreed.

She chuckled. "Wait until the next one. I hear there's supposed to be a wedding soon," she joked.

"Yeah." He sighed and moved slightly towards the doorway. "How about a walk?" he asked, turning back towards her.

She thought about it for a moment before nodding. With all of the bodies in the building and her running around, she was overheated. A walk on the beach would help cool her off before bed. She'd always found it difficult to shut down after a party. Normally, she'd take a walk herself, but after her sister's shooting, she'd stuck very close to the barn and her cottage.

After shutting all the lights off and making sure to lock up, she grabbed her jacket and followed him out into the night.

"Are you sure we're allowed?" she teased. Numerous times over the past few weeks he'd insisted on walking her home, each time reminding her that she shouldn't go out on her own.

"I think my uncle's right. I think Thomas Carson has decided to stick with legal methods of pissing my family off now," he said, putting his hands in the pockets of his leather jacket.

"Is it true that he tried to stop the construction by suing your uncle under a goat's name?" she asked.

"It was a donkey," he corrected with a chuckle. "Yes. If I'd been around, I would have had the case thrown out a lot quicker. Work wouldn't have stopped for a single day."

She stopped walking. "What? Why?"

He stopped and turned to her. "Because a donkey can't file an injunction," he said with a chuckle.

"No, I mean, how would you have stopped it?" She shook her head as she started walking again.

"I've only spent the last five years studying law," he countered.

Her steps faltered, and he reached out to steady her. She'd done everything over the past few weeks except talk to him about his life. The fact was, she didn't even really know anything about him. She'd assumed he was just as shallow as the women he paraded around.

"Law?" she asked. "I guess I didn't figure you for..." She stopped when she realized what she'd been about to say.

It was his turn to stop walking. "What?" he asked, looking at her. "A lawyer?"

"Nothing," she shook her head quickly.

"No, go on." His eyes searched hers, much like he'd been doing earlier, before he'd kissed her.

She realized how close they were to one another and stopped herself from taking a step back.

"I just…" She lost track of what she was saying since her eyes were locked on his. "I didn't think of you as the brainy type." She realized what she'd said after he started laughing. "I didn't mean…" She felt her face heat.

She closed her eyes with embarrassment. When she felt his hand on her back, she opened them again. He'd moved closer again and was less than a breath from her. She had a moment's warning before his lips covered hers again.

"Why?" she asked, once he pulled back slightly. She'd enjoyed the kiss as much as the first one and this time was thankful that she'd had a little more forewarning.

She'd been able to brace herself and prepare for the flood of pure lust that washed over her.

"As I mentioned, I only have a few more weeks here," he said with a shrug. "Why don't we enjoy ourselves while we can?"

She narrowed her eyes at him. What would it be like to be one of the women he paraded around? Would it be worth it? Something told her that physically, yes, it would. But could she allow her own reputation to be tarnished in town?

After all, his family had a strong hold on the small town. They were everywhere. They owned restaurants and businesses she relied on, like the flower shop. And his mother, Lacey, was the mayor of the town.

Remembering this, she took a step back.

"I don't think that's such a good idea." She let the realization sink in. There was no way she could afford to have a little fling with George. Not when her and her sister's business and her way of life could be on the line.

"Afraid?" he challenged with a smile.

"Of you? No. Of it jeopardizing my business and life, yes," she admitted. "I can't do complications at this time."

He was silent for a moment. "Okay, what if I could promise you that this"—he motioned between them—"whatever we have, stays between us and stays uncomplicated?"

She thought about it a moment. Thought about letting herself cut loose. For once in her life, letting herself take what she wanted. "I would need your word," she said quickly.

He nodded. "I can do that. My family pretty much leaves me alone. They've got it in their mind that I'm a lost cause."

"I wonder where they got that idea?" she said with a smile.

His smile grew as he stepped closer to her. "See, that's one of the reasons I'm drawn to you." Then his smile turned slightly. "Need me to draw up an agreement? Make it legal?"

She couldn't help the chuckle that escaped her. "I think that a verbal agreement will suffice." She held out her hand for his.

His hand wrapped around hers, and she noticed how much bigger it was than her own.

"There." His eyes moved to her lips again. "We'll just add a kiss to seal the deal," he said before kissing her.

This time, she allowed herself to enjoy and relax into his touch. His mouth moved over hers, and she felt her entire body vibrating with desire.

"So?" he asked when his lips released hers. "We have an accord."

Her eyes locked with his as she reached out and took his hand in hers and started walking towards the small cottage that she'd called home for over a year.

"This stays between us," she warned again for some reason.

His smile grew and he nodded again quickly as an answer.

She knew that she was probably making a mistake, but she no longer cared. She was going to enjoy herself while she could. Just as long as it didn't interfere with her work and didn't mess up her business.

There was no way she was going to let any man destroy her life ever again. Even if she had to protect her heart by hiding it away.

CHAPTER FOUR

How had he gotten so lucky? As Robin led him towards her cottage, his mind was so preoccupied with thoughts of being with her, he couldn't see anything else.

He'd enjoyed that she'd challenged him in many ways, including questioning his intellect. After all, he'd witnessed her intelligence firsthand. Even though her business was an easy one, it still took brains to make it all work.

He knew that her younger sister was the heart of the business, while Robin was the brains. He'd seen her business diploma from the University of Oregon hanging up in her small office near the back of the barn.

Robin pulled him in the front door of the small cottage. He'd been in the two-bedroom place several times. He and his cousins had been friends with the previous owner's son, but he hadn't seen all the remodeling that had been done since Robin had moved in.

Robin didn't give him any time to appreciate what she'd done to the place or even enough time to see how she'd redecorated. Instead, she'd pulled him down the hallway towards her bedroom.

When she shut the door behind him, he pulled her into his arms and kissed her until they both came away a little breathless.

He wanted to say something to her, but the next moment she stepped back and stripped off her coat, and he lost the ability to speak. Then she started slowly unbuttoning her shirt and his mouth went completely dry. She tossed it away, leaving her standing in front of him in a sexy white silk bra.

Her skin was flawless. Flushed, creamy white, and so beautiful that he couldn't help but want to enjoy her slowly.

"Perfect," he heard himself saying as he reached out and brushed the back of his hand down her shoulder.

Stepping away, she tugged off her slacks quickly. Then she leaned in and pushed his coat off his shoulders and started unbuttoning his shirt. Reaching down, he helped her remove it and then tossed it down on the floor along with hers.

Her eyes ran over him, and he allowed her a moment like he'd taken to enjoy her. Just as he had done, she reached up and ran her hand over his bare skin.

Closing his eyes, he moaned with desire as he appreciated her soft touch.

"Wow, if I'd known what was hiding under there, I would have gotten your clothes off you long ago," she purred as she stepped closer to him.

"I feel the same way," he said, pulling her up against

him until they were skin to skin. The only barrier left was the silk she wore.

This time the kiss was more demanding, and he felt his own urgency and desires grow as his hands roamed over her body. He'd known she would be a tight little package. After all, he'd seen her in enough sexy outfits over the past few weeks to appreciate the view.

Now, however, he was getting to enjoy feeling every soft subtle curve she had. Just as she was running her hands over him. When she reached for his jeans, he backed her up until her knees hit the side of her bed.

"Let me," he said as she sat down on the edge of the bed. Taking his time, he stepped back and slowly pulled his shoes and his jeans off. He left his boxers on and made a point to stick the condom he kept in his wallet on her nightstand.

When he stepped closer to her again, her hands moved up and wrapped around his waist as he kissed her again.

Lifting her into his arms, he held onto her as she wrapped her legs around his hips.

"George," she said as he trailed his mouth down her neck, "please."

He smiled and buried his face into her hair. "Hold onto me," he said, turning until he sat on the edge of the bed with her on his lap.

The way she was moving over him, grinding him, he knew that it wouldn't be long before he'd lose the last little bit of the hold that he had on his control.

He shifted and felt her jump slightly when he

cupped her sex. Lifting her, he flipped her down on the mattress. He needed to get a taste of her.

"I want to enjoy you," he said, trailing his mouth down her shoulders. Pushing the silky bra aside, he sucked her nipple until she cried out his name.

He rained little kisses over her skin as he moved lower, dipping the tip of his tongue into her belly button, enjoying the sweet taste of her.

When he reached the top of her matching silk panties, he ran his mouth over them as her fingers tangled in his hair.

"George." His name was more of a warning. "I can't." She shook her head. He smiled up at her as he slipped the silk material down and then off her legs.

Running his eyes over her, he held in a slight groan at her beauty.

"I said it before but it's true—you're a picture of perfection." He slowly ran his hand over her. This time when he cupped her, she cried out his name and arched into his hand.

He slipped a finger into her heat, and she gripped the comforter as soft sexy moans egged him on further. Dipping his head down, he settled between her legs and tasted her. He'd never had anything sweeter in his life and thought he might have said so as he lost himself in her pleasure.

When he felt her release and tasted her on his tongue, he slipped on the condom and then moved up and settled between her thighs.

"Look at me, Robin," he said as he moved over her.

Her eyes fluttered open slowly, and he waited until

they focused on him. They he slipped into her and lost part of himself.

"YOU HAVE TO GO," Robin said, shaking him awake.

"Hm?" He wrapped his arms around her and pulled her down to bury his face in her soft hair.

"George," she hissed, "my sister's going to be here soon."

His eyes opened wide. "She is? Why on earth?" he asked.

She shrugged. "She claims she forgot a few cookbooks in the kitchen. She wants them since she's making a special meal for Conner." She pulled out of his arms and wiggled her cell phone.

It was then that he noticed she'd pulled on a pair of sweats and a T-shirt.

He glanced around for his own phone to see what time it was.

"It's almost six," Robin said, as if she'd read his mind.

"In the morning?" he balked.

"Yes," she hissed, and nudged him again as he rolled towards her. "You have to go."

He shook his head. "Can't I just... hide out in here until she's gone?"

"No." She shook her head. "You promised."

Groaning, he shoved the thought of repeating last night's pleasure to the back of his mind as he hunted for his clothes. When Robin handed him his pants, he pulled them on quickly.

Just before heading out her door, he pulled her into

his arms and kissed her until he felt her melt against him again.

"Tonight?" he asked.

"I'll text you," she replied, and shoved him out the door. "Now go." She shut the door in his face.

He chuckled all the way to his car. As he pulled onto the main street, he noticed Kara's new car, which Conner had helped her purchase, heading towards him. So she wouldn't think that he'd just pulled out of their place, he parked in front of his cousin's flower shop, All in Bloom. He glanced up at the old brick building.

The flower shop was in the middle of three units. One unit was currently a hair salon and the other had at one point been a real estate office. It was now sitting empty and had a for rent sign in the window.

He remembered being in there years ago and could vaguely recall what it looked like inside.

His mind ran over the possibilities as he turned off the engine and climbed out to take a better look through the windows, just to refresh his memory.

The more he looked at it, the more he realized that it would be perfect for a small legal office. He could see clearly through the windows and confirmed that there was still a small receptionist area out front. He remembered there being an office in the back with a full conference room directly across the hallway. He even thought there might be a storeroom or break room of some sort off the back with a door that led to the alley behind the buildings.

How long had he been dreaming of moving back to Pride, even though he knew there wasn't really a need for a lawyer in such a small town? His family's lawyer was from Edgeview, the closest city. Most of the people in Pride used law firms from the city, which is why he doubted he could make it in his hometown.

Still, that didn't stop him from dreaming.

Stepping back, he almost bumped into his cousin Suzie.

"I thought that was you." She smiled up at him. "What are you doing out of bed this early in the morning?" she asked him, then narrowed her eyes quickly. "Did you get kicked out of someone's bed?"

He chuckled as an answer. "How much are they asking for rent?" He redirected her easily enough.

Suzie glanced over at the storefront. "Thinking of opening a boutique?" she teased.

"How much?" He tugged on the end of her hair playfully.

"Well, if you want to come in, we can call Kathy together and find out." She motioned to the front door of her flower shop.

Since he was committed to not looking like a fool, he followed his cousin into the store. While Suzie dug out Kathy's number, he glanced around at all the pretty flowers and vases she had and wondered if he should send Robin something nice.

Hadn't he promised her last night that they would keep it uncomplicated? Then why, for the first time ever, was he thinking of getting a woman flowers?

He shook off those thoughts, when his cousin gave him the cell phone number of the owner of the building, Kathy Bernard.

Hearing the small monthly amount that Kathy wanted for the place, he almost convinced himself that he could pull it off. When Kathy said that she'd give him a week to think it over, he hung up and almost persuaded himself to give her an answer right then and there.

When he left Suzie's store, he had a bundle of flowers tucked under his arm for his mother. If he moved back into town and opened his own practice, could he get enough business in Pride to sustain a life?

The rest of his cousins were having homes built in Hidden Cove. Could he afford something like that himself if he stayed?

If he added in the rent of the building, the cost for some basic renovations, the expense of a receptionist, he could probably afford a place in the new neighborhood. It was, at least, worth a drive out to take a look at the homes. If he was going to indulge in the fantasy, he might as well go full force.

And since there weren't any events happening at the venue until later that afternoon, he figured after grabbing some homemade breakfast—

"What are you doing?" His mother's voice stopped him in his tracks just a few steps through the front door. He knew that tone. That was the same tone he used to get when he tracked in mud after she'd spent a full day preparing the house for company.

Instantly, he glanced down at his shoes and winced when he noticed he'd tracked in a few drops of rainwater.

Instead of answering her, he held out the bundle of flowers.

His mother's eyes narrowed at him as she took them

and held them up to her face. After taking in a deep breath of their scent, she pointed a finger at him.

"You're just coming in," she accused him. "From?"

Shit. He hadn't thought of a lie about where he'd spent last night. If he was going to keep his word to Robin, his family couldn't know anything.

"Getting you those from Suzie's place," he said quickly and noticed his mother's eyes narrow again. "And from talking to Kathy about renting the empty unit next to Suzie's shop."

This had his mother's eyes popping wide open in question.

"You're thinking of moving back to Pride?" she asked. He could tell she was no longer thinking about whether he'd spent the night somewhere else. Instead, she was focused on him moving back home, permanently.

"I'm thinking about it," he admitted, not wanting to own up to the fact that it was just a quick thought but not one he could take too seriously.

"It's about damn time," his mother said, walking back to the kitchen to put the flowers in water. Before she got too far, she turned and glared down at his feet.

George was no fool. He quickly removed his shoes and set them by the front door before following her inside the rest of the way.

"Pride could use a good lawyer. Everyone has been complaining ever since Ed Sharp retired a few years back that there isn't one in town." His mother took her time filling up a vase and arranging the flowers.

"Really?" He sat on the barstool and watched her. "I

thought everyone was content getting legal help from Edgeview."

"No." His mother glanced over at him. "Even Todd was complaining about it the other day when he had to file some paperwork. Not that he minds using Josh Scott out of Edgeview, but..." She shook her head. "It does get old driving all the way to Edgeview just to sign papers. Besides, we didn't put you through law school not to enjoy some of the benefits."

"If I move back to Pride, you might have to pay for my services like the rest of the townspeople."

His mother set the vase down in front of him and shook her head, putting her hand on her hips. "You'd charge your own mother?"

He chuckled, then walked over and wrapped his arms around her, marveling instantly at how very small but powerful she was. "Don't worry. I'll give you the family discount," he answered quickly. The statement earned him a poke in the ribs.

CHAPTER FIVE

Having her sister hang around the cottage for the entire day used to be a joy. However, on only a few hours of sleep, and needing time to think about the night before, the longer Kara hung around, the more irritable she felt.

By lunchtime, Robin finally got out of her sister the story of why Kara was hanging around all day.

"So, that's why Conner wanted me to hang around with you all day," Kara explained.

"Because he saw a couple of strange men hanging around town last night?" Robin asked.

"Yeah." Kara rolled her eyes. "Something tells me that every time a stranger comes into town, we're going to be watched over."

She thought about George and wondered if he knew about the men last night. If that had anything to do with why he'd stayed with her. No. Whatever last night had been about, George hadn't been thinking about protecting her. That much was true.

Last night had been all about lust. About release.

She'd needed it as much as he had. They'd been skirting around one another for over a month and last night was the result of that flirting.

Her sister helped her set up for the birthday party on the schedule for later that evening before heading out to make her special dinner for Conner. Kara's left arm was still in a sling, but she knew that her sister was well enough to help straighten the chairs and to set the vases of flowers on each table.

An hour before the birthday guests were due to arrive, George showed up. She hadn't seen him yet, but she'd noticed his car out front. He was probably outside, making his rounds around the property to ensure that no one was hiding in the shadows.

She hoped that he planned on staying with her again that night. When she'd woken in his arms, she'd wished more than anything that the text message from her sister hadn't woken her and that she'd have an entire morning to enjoy the sexy muscular body she was up against.

Just thinking about it, she found herself scanning the barn for a glimpse of him. When her eyes landed on him, a smile curved her lips up and, as if he'd felt it, his eyes moved over to land on her. His instant smile matched hers.

Then the party guests started arriving, and she became so busy that she didn't have time to think about their time together the night before or worry if he'd stick around after the party to be with her again.

So much had gone into her business, and she knew that she couldn't afford to be distracted. Not for long. Having fun couldn't get in the way of her business.

Period. Still, she had a libido and after last night, just knowing what sex was like with George, what it could be like, desire flooded her quickly.

The sweet-sixteen birthday party seemed to go by in slow motion. She'd outdone herself on the decorations for the young Ester Ellison, or Essie as all of her friends called her. The massive barn was decked out in pale pink decorations with Edison lights hanging overhead, and boys and girls danced to the latest songs played by her favorite DJ, Brett Lyons. She used Brett for all of the parties that required music. She liked the young guy and knew that he'd graduated from high school the previous year and was working part time down at the Golden Oar as a waiter.

There were a handful of people in Pride that she relied on to keep her business running smoothly. She'd be totally lost if it wasn't for the kitchen crew. Joy Smith, the head chef Robin had hired two weeks after they'd open their doors, had been one of her best hires. A few of the other kitchen staff came and went, but Joy was steady.

The older woman knew how to manage the other employees, and Robin only needed to pass the client's requested menu on to Joy to ensure that it would be done.

Her sister had made sure that all the flower orders had been delivered, so that was another thing she hadn't had to worry about. Actually, the more Robin thought about it, the hardest part of the business was the cleanup.

Sunset Weddings, or Sunset Venue, as most people were now calling it, had earned its reputation as one of the swankiest and most unique barn venues on the

Oregon coast. To Robin's knowledge, it was the only barn venue that overlooked the Pacific Ocean.

They were completely booked every Friday and Saturday night until next fall, which ensured her that she'd made the right career choice.

It had been a hardship leaving the city. She'd really liked the hustle and bustle of city life. But she'd never been a partier and hadn't really liked driving on the over-crowded streets.

What she had liked was being able to entertain herself with friends and family. Family that was now living just a few blocks from her. Well, at least half of that family. Her cousins and her aunt and uncle were still in Portland. But the important people were there, with them.

When her parents walked into the party less than half an hour after the event started, she wished more than anything to be back in the city. To have a little more privacy again. She was hoping to have the evening alone with George and, once again, her family would be the reason that didn't happen.

"Mom, Dad, what are you doing here?" She met them at the door.

Both of her parents were smiling and looking around. "We were invited," her mother said before waving to Joseline Ellison, Essie's mother.

"Josie and I go way back," her mother said easily. "Don't worry about us, we're just here to enjoy the party and give Essie our best." She motioned to the large gift her father was carrying in his hands.

Okay, it was going to take some getting used to, seeing

her parents around town constantly. She loved them and enjoyed being around them, but seeing them reminded her that business should come above all else and made her feel guilty for recent distractions. After all, they were the ones who put her through school and helped her and Kara after their grandfather died and left them their inheritance to purchase this very property.

She owed them a lot. They were the reason she and her sister believed that happy-ever-afters could come after wedding bells.

For the rest of the evening, she kept herself busy refilling the punch bowl and the sandwich platters, or just making sure kids didn't sneak off somewhere and make out.

Which is what she was doing when George found her up in the loft after catching the birthday girl and her on again, off again boyfriend, Evan. She'd interrupted a very heated season of making out and only had to motion to the stairs to get the young couple scurrying away.

A low chuckle moments later caused her to jump slightly and spin around.

"You know, I bet there was a time when you snuck off like that yourself," George said, stepping into the light.

Her eyes narrowed. "Were you standing there the entire time?"

He chuckled and shook his head as he moved closer to her. "No, just got up here as the young couple was headed down. But I can imagine why they were up here in the first place." His arms wrapped around her hips and pulled her closer. "Which has me thinking..." His lips brushed against hers.

She felt her legs turn to jelly as she held onto him. "George." She sighed when he pulled back and started running his mouth down her neck. "I... We can't."

"I know," he said against her skin. "But since no one is looking, we can take just a moment." He kissed her again before releasing her and taking a full step backwards. She felt wobbly and reached out for the railing to steady herself.

"What are you doing tomorrow?" he asked suddenly.

She frowned. Mondays were normally slow days, which allowed her to catch up on her paperwork and orders.

She opened her mouth to tell him just that but shrugged instead. "Nothing that can't be moved around. Why?"

He smiled. "I was going to take the boat out for the first time this year."

Her eyebrows shot up. "Sailing?"

He nodded. "It's sort of a family pastime. I've been going out on the water since before I was born, or so my parents tell me." He chuckled. "What do you say we make a day of it?"

She thought about the cool weather. About being out on the water in what was still almost dead winter in Oregon. She'd only ever been on a boat a handful of times and that had been in the heat of summer.

"Won't the weather put a damper on the day?" she asked.

"No." His smile grew and then he took a deep breath. "Actually, this is one of my favorite times of year to be out on the water. The bite of the air, the crispness of it." He glanced down as a loud burst of laughter sounded from below. "I was going to head out around eight. I'll pack breakfast and lunch, and we'll be back before dinnertime."

"Why not," she heard herself saying. "What should I wear?"

He chuckled. "Something warm."

She nodded as they started walking towards the stairs. "Can I bring anything?"

"If you have a wine you like," he said after a moment. "I'll handle everything else." He glanced at her, and her heart did a little flip as his eyes ran over her lips. "I'd like to kiss you again, but I'll wait until we're alone."

For the rest of the evening, she was walking on air. She tried to keep George off her mind, but each time she found a moment alone to think, there he was, popping up in her thoughts again.

"So." Her mother stopped beside her as she sipped a glass of juice. "What's between you and George Stevens?"

It was a good thing Robin hadn't been taking a sip of the juice right then because, as it was, she started choking on air. She could only imagine what would have happened if she'd had a mouth full of juice.

Her mother reached over and slapped her softly on the back a few times until Robin recovered.

"What makes you ask that?" she asked once she could breathe again.

Her mother laughed. "I'm not blind or stupid."

"Nothing," Robin sighed. "Nothing is going on between me and George. Not really."

Her mother tilted her head as her eyes ran over her face. "Don't get me wrong. I've known George his entire life. I can remember the two of you playing, along with all the other kids, almost every year of your lives. He's a good man. A smart one." Her mother's eyes narrowed. "But I also know that he's gained a reputation in recent years as a man who won't be tied down."

"Mom." She rolled her eyes. "I have my business. I'm not looking to tie anyone down. I'm too busy. If there is anything between me and anyone"—she drew that last word out—"believe me, I'm not looking for it to last. Not at this point in my life."

Her mother seemed to relax at this. "I don't approve of one-night stands, and I know you're smart enough to protect—"

Robin groaned, and her mother chuckled.

"I'll leave it at that." Her mother touched her arm and then squeezed lightly. "Great party by the way. Really great party. I'm so very proud of you and your sister for this place." She glanced around. "It's one of the most romantic places." She chuckled. "Even for a sweet-sixteen party." Her mother leaned in and placed a soft kiss on her cheek. "Your dad and I are going to head home."

"I'll walk you out." She took her mother's hand. "I could use some fresh air."

When she followed her parents outside and took in the crisp night air, she knew instantly what George had been talking about. Just feeling the cold breeze wash over her made her feel more alive. Bolder somehow.

She thought about tomorrow. Thought about what

she was going to wear, what it meant that he wanted to spend the day with her. They'd made an agreement to keep things light and to keep what was between them away from others.

Of course, they'd only made that agreement a day ago and her mother had already guessed what was between them. Would others guess as easily? Had she made a mistake in agreeing to being with him?

Then her mind played over what he'd done to her last night, what they had done to one another, and a slow smile curved her lips. Whatever it had been, she wouldn't call it a mistake.

"We should do this more often," Emma said, moving to stand beside her, causing her to jump slightly. Emma Auston was a vibrant redhead who had skin like a porcelain doll and energy like the nineteen-year-old she was.

"Hm?" she asked, wrapping her arms around herself to ward off the chill.

"Sweet-sixteen parties," Emma answered with a smile. "Maybe we can make it a regular thing. Spend some money advertising at the high school? I know a lot of girls I went to school with would have loved having their parties here."

"I'd thought the same thing," Robin admitted. "Next time we'll have to request more chaperones though."

"Agreed." Emma chuckled. "I've caught five couples making out in dark corners. I never knew there were so many of them around this place." Emma shook her head, then leaned closer to her. "One of the couples happened to be your parents." She nodded to where her parents' car taillights had just disappeared down the drive."

"Seriously?" Robin laughed.

"Why do you think they left early?" Emma chuckled as she walked away.

"Thanks for that imagery. I won't be able to get it out of my head now," she called after her.

"That makes two of us," Emma called back.

Deciding she needed another moment, she stood out on the patio and took several deep breaths until she felt a little more relaxed and in control. At least in her head.

Tomorrow, well, she was just going to enjoy what came. No matter what it was.

CHAPTER SIX

George couldn't count how many times over the years that he'd been out on the water in his family's sailboat.

He knew what he needed to bring for a good day out on the water.

He tried not to think about how it would be the first time he'd taken a woman out on the family boat or that, after promising to keep things light with Robin, a full-day date could be crossing that line.

Instead, his mind was consumed with being with her again. Enjoying that tight, soft body of hers, appreciating the way she moved up against him.

He thought of that as he packed everything that they would need in the sailboat named *Dawn-Treader II*. It was named after the smaller vessel that had gone down the day George's grandfather, the man he was named after, had perished and his uncle Iian had lost his hearing.

He could remember the first time he'd gone out on the small single-mast cutter. He remembered because, that day, he'd fallen in love with sailing.

It had been his uncle Todd and cousin, Matthew who had taken him out on the water first. He must have been around eight and, from that day forward, he'd begged his uncle each weekend to take him sailing again. He had, of course, and had shown him the ropes.

He stashed the food in the small kitchen below deck and started prepping for the day. When Robin showed up, everything was ready.

"Morning," he said with a smile as he held out a hand for her to climb aboard.

She looked down at it and smiled. "Isn't there some sort of rule that I have to ask for permission to come aboard?"

His smile doubled. "Permission granted." He reached across the space, placed his hands on her hips, and carted her across as he covered her lips with his. "Morning," he said again.

"Mmm," she sighed against him, then glanced around. "Show me around?"

He nodded and released her, then quickly held her hips when she swayed with the boat.

"Sorry," she mumbled.

"It takes a while to grow into your sea legs," he explained. "Until then, you can sit or hold onto the railing. This"—he motioned around— "is the *Dawn-Treader Two*."

"Two?" she asked with a frown. "What happened to the first one? Did it sink?" she asked, concern flooding her voice.

"It did," he answered. "Over thirty years ago, during a terrible storm. Taking my grandfather"—he leaned towards her slightly— "the man I'm named after, with it."

"I'm sorry," she said softly. Then she snapped her finger. "Your uncle. Is that how Iian lost his hearing?" He nodded. "I think I heard the story when I first moved into town. Your grandfather sacrificed his life for your uncle's life."

"Yeah." He nodded with a sigh. "My aunt's painting of the first *Dawn-Treader* is hanging in the Golden Oar."

"I've admired the painting." She glanced around and seemed to relax. "So, how long have you been sailing?"

"Since I was eight. Or around there. My uncle Todd taught me. I can't remember a summer I didn't spend countless hours out on the water. Every Jordan knows how to sail." He motioned. "The galley." He opened the small door that led down the narrow stairs. "Bathroom, kitchen, bedroom." He wiggled his eyebrows and gained a smile from her. "But for now..." He walked over and lifted up a life vest and handed it to her. "Until we get out on open water. Family rules."

She took the vest from him and easily put it on over her jacket.

"There's coffee." He grabbed the cups he'd stopped at Sara's Nook to get earlier. "It's probably still a little warm. And there are fresh baked goods." He handed her the coffee and then held out the bakery box.

Taking a muffin for himself, he moved over to the start the motor.

"Any questions?" he asked as she moved over and sat down to eat her muffin and sip her coffee while he finished untying the lines.

"Lots," she said, watching his every movement. "But the first question is, should I expect to get wet?"

He chuckled. "No, not unless you decide to jump in the water," he said, between sips of coffee and eating the rest of his muffin.

Using the motor, he slowly steered them out of the harbor. He knew that if they had started out earlier, they would have been in line to get out of the narrow inlet. Fishing boats usually headed out around five in the morning and would normally return back to Pride Harbor somewhere after noon.

"Aren't you going to use those?" Robin asked, motioning towards the sails. She held her coffee mug between her hands, using its heat to stay warm.

"Not until we get out on the open water. It's easier to maneuver inside the harbor with the motor." He motioned with his free hand. "There's a blanket," he started.

"I'm fine." She shook her head. "It's like you said, it makes you feel... alive." She turned her face up to the sky. "What's that called?" she asked him, motioning overhead with her free hand.

"That's the mainsail. The one in the front is called the headsail," he answered her.

"That's the mast?" she asked, motioning again.

"Yes." He nodded. "See, you're already more knowledgeable than most. You'll have your sea legs in no time. Just wait and see," he joked.

For the next half hour, as they slowly made their way out to the wide openness of the Pacific, he taught her all about the boat and about sailing.

She helped him unroll the sails, and when they filled with wind and the small vessel took off, she laughed and held onto him as they jutted across the water.

He showed her how to steer and how to keep from knocking herself or anyone else out with the boom when the sailboat changed directions. He let her take the helm for a while, and he could tell that she really enjoyed having control.

For several hours, they followed the wind up the Oregon coast. When they grew hungry, he lowered the sails and tossed the anchor overboard so that they floated in a small, secluded cove.

"I don't think I've ever realized how beautiful the coast of Oregon is. I mean, I've enjoyed the views from Highway One, but seeing it from out here..." She leaned against the railing and released a soft sigh. "Wow," she said, glancing over at him.

Her cheeks and the tip of her nose were slightly pink from the chill. She'd worn a pair of dark gray jeans and a black-and-white striped shirt under a white coat, which she'd unzipped when she'd helped him drop anchor. She had a white hat that covered most of her long hair, which was lying over her shoulder in a thick braid. She had a pair of sunglasses on, and he wished he could see her eyes.

He followed her gaze and had to agree about the views. Tall rocky cliffs seemed to hang over the water's edge in places with patches of rolling grassy hills in between. An occasional farm or small cluster of homes dotted the landscape.

But for the most part, it was the complete wilderness

and isolation of the countryside that took his breath away and always had.

He stood next to Robin and debated wrapping his arm around her waist so he could pull her closer to him. He knew that she wanted to keep what was between them from everyone else, but he didn't know if that meant she didn't want to have any kind of relationship outside of sex.

When she leaned against his chest, he smiled and relaxed as he held her.

"Thank you," she said, glancing up at him.

"For?" he asked, enjoying the way the sunlight touched her braided hair and highlighted little streaks of red in the long tresses.

"Today. I can't remember the last time I had a full day off to myself." She smiled. "I suppose I needed it."

"When you work hard, you deserve to play just as hard," he said with a shrug. It had been the number one philosophy in his life, which was one of the reasons that he always had a new woman on his arm. He'd talked himself into believing he deserved it. He'd always believed that with so many different flavors of women out there, he had an obligation to sample as many as he could so that one day he'd be able to decide what exactly it was that he wanted.

"Yes." She smiled and turned away. "Your reputation for playing hard proceeds you."

He winced slightly and decided to change the subject.

"How about some lunch?" he asked.

She chuckled softly but agreed. She followed him

down the narrow stairs into the lower room. He'd spent countless summers living out of the sailboat with a few of his family members. One summer, he and his cousin Matt had spent weeks sailing down the coast to San Diego before turning around and coming back home.

At the end of the three weeks, he'd been thankful to have his privacy again. Of course, that was the summer he'd decided to become a lawyer after his cousin complained that he argued like one.

Robin asked to help him, but he knew there wasn't enough room in the kitchen for two people.

"You sit." He motioned to the small table. "Normally, we'd eat up on deck, but it's warmer down here since the wind kicked up."

"I'm not complaining." She removed her jacket. His mouth started watering when he noticed just how her shirt clung to her curves. He was so distracted that he almost dumped the plate of sandwiches onto the floor.

"Focus," she said with a slight chuckle as she took the plate from his hands.

"It's kind of hard to when you're wearing skintight clothes." He felt his entire body react to seeing her nipples poke through the thin material. "My god." He shook his head. "What was I saying?"

She chuckled again. "Food first," she warned when he reached for her. "I worked up an appetite steering the boat."

He chuckled. "Okay, food first." He walked over and grabbed a bag of chips and some drinks and set them down on the table before sitting next to her.

"So, tell me. How many times have you taken other women sailing?" she asked.

Shit, he thought. If he told her he'd never taken anyone else out sailing, how would that make him look? Desperate? Would she believe this meant more than it did?

"Not a lot of women would trust me with their lives," he said casually with a shrug.

"So"—she glanced over at him— "no one else?"

He could hear the worry in the tone. Worry and something else he couldn't figure out.

"It's not like I haven't taken plenty of others out on the water." He tried for casual. "Just not anyone I've... slept with before."

She relaxed slightly. "Okay, so, what do you normally do with women you're... dating?"

"Is that what this is?" he asked, motioning between them.

She glanced sideways at him. "No," she answered quickly with a shrug. "I don't have time for dating, or beyond."

"Beyond?" he asked, holding in a chuckle. "Funny. I thought that was what we did the other night."

She smiled quickly. "Sex is sex. Dating is... complicated, and beyond..." She rolled her eyes. "I deal with the beyond every day at work." She leaned a little closer to him. "I'm years away from the beyond." She tilted her head and then chuckled. "And, from what I hear about you, you are centuries away from the beyond."

That stung a little. He didn't know why, but there it was. He always figured he'd eventually get the nerve to settle down. After all, part of him deep down wanted the beyond and everything that came with it. The wife, a home with a white picket fence, a yard where kids and dogs would play.

It was just a matter of finding the right woman. Wasn't it?

"What about you?" He watched her eyebrows shoot up in question. "Why did you pick weddings?"

"It was Kara's idea," she said quickly. "Although, we'd always had a fascination with weddings. What little girl didn't that grew up with parents that were... well, had the perfect marriage." She shrugged as she finished her sandwich. "We both wanted to see others celebrate their happiness."

"It's rough," he said, causing her to look at him again. "Growing up under the influence of a happy couple. Their happiness casts a large shadow over everyone else. It almost makes you feel like you're required to find that perfect person to spend the rest of your life with."

"The hunt for someone to love," she said softly.

He chuckled. "I suppose it is a kind of hunt."

"You have a reputation for being an excellent hunter," she added with a smile.

He laughed. "Jealous?"

"Don't get me wrong," she said, holding up her wine glass for him to pour her more from the bottle she'd brought along. "I've gone on a few hunting excursions myself." She rolled her eyes. "A few I'd like to forget."

"Oh?" he asked, finishing off his lunch. "Care to share the stories?"

"The last one put me off expecting..."

"The beyond?" he jumped in.

"Yeah," she said with a sigh. "So when Kara suggested we start our own business, we pooled our inheritance together and jumped at the chance to purchase the barn. We'd been coming to Pride all our lives, and I remember one winter our dad took us to a hayride that the man who owned the barn had going for the holidays."

"The Rogers," he added. "They used to run the hayride every Christmas. When it snowed, they had a sled."

"Yes." She smiled. "It was snowing that year, and I remember walking into the barn and thinking how magical the place was. How... romantic."

"How old were you?"

"Ten, eleven." She shrugged.

He thought about what he'd been doing at that age. He'd most likely still been in torn jeans, chasing his cousins around playing tag football with no thought to girls or romance. He guessed it was true that boys matured later than girls. He'd always figured he had such a sex drive in the past few years because he'd gotten a late start.

CHAPTER SEVEN

Robin noticed the change in George when she mentioned romance and instantly regretted bringing it up. She should have known better. They'd made the agreement to keep this, whatever it actually was between them, light.

"So." She decided to change the subject quickly as she set down the last of her drink. "Exactly how are we going to get back if the wind is blowing us up the coast instead of down?"

He chuckled and moved a little closer to her, and then wrapped his arm around her shoulders. She felt her heart kick hard in her chest as her body pressed up against his.

His eyes ran over her face and landed on her lips. She fought the urge to lick her lips in anticipation.

"A sailor's secret," he whispered, before kissing her.

She couldn't help melting against his chest. Her arms reached up and wrapped around his shoulders as he leaned her back against the cushions.

She heard his elbow connect with the table and held in a chuckle as a low curse escaped him.

"Come with me," he said, scooting out of the bench. He held out his hand for hers.

Smiling, she allowed him to pull her up and over to the queen-sized mattress tucked at the very front of the boat. There were two small circular windows on either side of the bed, letting in daylight through sheer white curtains.

He laid her gently down on the bed, and she sighed as his hands roamed slowly over her while he took her mouth again.

It wasn't as if they had been rushed the first time, but knowing they had all the time in the world somehow made her appreciate the slowness even more. Besides, he seemed to enjoy taking his time exploring her. Pleasing her.

As he peeled off each layer of her clothes, his hands and mouth ran over her freshly exposed skin. She felt like a jumbled bundle of nerves as she tugged and pulled his clothing from him. Just seeing his perfect chest and arms had her entire body going on alert in anticipation of enjoying every inch of him.

How had she not burst into flames that first time? George was one of those men she'd admired from afar for years while dreaming of what it would be like to gain his attention. Now that she had it, had him, she wasn't quite sure what to do.

Thankfully, he seemed to know exactly what to do with her. Leaning back with a moan, her eyes closed as he traced her ribs with his mouth.

"God, I love the taste of you," he said against her skin. His breath had goose bumps rising over the spot.

"George." She reached up and tangled her fingers in his hair. "Please, I..."

"Tell me what you want," George said, glancing up at her. "Is it... this?" he asked as he traced a finger over her flat belly.

She sucked in her breath and smiled at him.

"Or this?" he asked as his finger moved lower while his eyes locked with hers.

The smile on her lips fell away as his finger traced the elastic of the lace panties that she'd worn with his pleasure in mind.

Her eyes closed as he traced the material that covered her.

"Do you like it when I do this?" he asked, focusing his attention on the material that covered her pussy.

A low moan escaped her lips as she arched into his hand. She heard him chuckle softly as he continued to play with the silk covering her.

"Please," she begged again. "I..." She closed her eyes tightly as he continued his exploration. When he nudged the material aside, she cried out with delight as he slipped a finger over her bare skin. When he dipped a finger into her, her shoulders bounded off the mattress.

She couldn't remember ever reacting to anyone like this before. Sure, sex had always been fun, but this... with George, was... staggering.

"That's it, come for me, Robin," he said as he kissed her inner thigh, then moved closer to cover her pussy with his mouth. "I want to taste you," he said a moment before lights exploded behind her eyelids, and she felt her body give him everything he'd asked for.

"I'm no longer in control of my body," she said with a sigh as he moved slowly up her.

She heard him chuckle a moment before he slipped slowly into her.

"Good, then let me take the helm," he said, coming up to her. Her eyes locked with his as she wrapped her legs around his hips.

She wanted to tell him how wonderful he made her feel. Wanted to explain to him how much it meant to her, but fear had her biting her lips instead.

"You're so perfect," he said against her ear. "You feel so damn good," he whispered, sending another wave of goose bumps over her skin.

Her nails scraped lightly over his sides as he moved. She matched his pace, his speed now, and knew that as he built her up once more, she would gladly let him take the helm anytime he wanted.

"It's getting late," he said after their bodies had cooled off. She could still feel the bite of the chill in the air, but the soft rocking of the boat had lulled her, as had the glorious numbness of the aftermath of mind-blowing sex.

"Mmm," was her only reply. She doubted she could put together more than two words at this point.

Then George moved, and she felt the bitter coldness of the evening air hit her. She reached out for his warmth and cracked an eye open to find him.

She realized instantly that it had grown so much darker in the cabin and guessed that they must have both fallen asleep for a while.

Worry about how they would get back home surfaced.

Sitting up slowly, she looked around for her clothes and quickly pulled on her shirt when George handed it to her.

"What time is it?" she asked, hunting the small space for her jeans.

"A little past three," he said, tugging on his own jeans.

"Three?" How had it gotten so late?

"Yeah, I guess we both needed the rest," he said with a slight shrug as his eyes ran over her. Then he slowly smiled as he pinned her down by placing his hands on either side of her on the mattress. His eyebrows wiggled slightly as he added, "And the rest."

Smiling, she pulled him in for a kiss. "I wish we could just stay here for the night and head back in the morning."

"Next time," he promised. "I'll make sure to pack enough supplies. But now, we'd better start back."

She slipped on the rest of her clothes and stood up to pull on her coat.

"How? Will we use the sails?" she asked.

"It depends," he answered. "If we have a northern wind."

"If not?" She followed him up the narrow stairs.

"The motor will get us back safely." He glanced up at the mast.

She followed his gaze and for the first time since she'd stepped onto the boat, noticed a small white flag at the very top.

"Looks like we're in luck," he said with a smile. "The winds changed while we were below."

She could feel it for herself. Earlier, the wind coming from the south had been a warm, steady breeze. Now, however, it was driving down from the north in almost mad gusts that bit at her skin and was a lot colder than before. She pulled her jacket tighter around her and shoved the hat back on her head, then she helped George hoist the anchor and open the sails, and he steered the sailboat back down the coast.

This time, she sat directly next to him and leaned into him for his warmth as they watched the shoreline pass by quickly on the opposite side of the boat. She covered herself with the blanket for extra warmth since the air had become downright chilly.

As the sun sank lower in the sky, she watched the colors wash over the hills and rocks of the coast. She jumped up and took several pictures when they spotted a pod of whales, then turned her camera on George as he stood at the helm, legs spread wide like a true sailor as he steered. His black hat and old wool coat reminded her of an old black-and-white movie about a sailor falling madly in love with a mermaid.

The romantic in her wanted to enjoy the moment, but then a gust of wind washed right through her, and she was back huddling under the blanket and wrapped in his warm arms.

As they headed back down the coast, they talked about family and their jobs as the beautiful coastal scenery passed by them until the sky grew dark enough that the view was dulled.

When he mentioned he was thinking of renting the unit next to Suzie's flower shop, she was slightly surprised.

"I didn't think you were going to stick around town," she said, trying to hide the interest and excitement about the possibility of having a little bit longer with him.

She had known that to save herself from heartbreak she'd have to demand they keep things light between them.

Besides, with his reputation, she'd been wise to understand what she was getting herself into in the first place. George was a player. That had been clear from the first moment she'd overheard him calling his date last year by the wrong name.

"I hadn't really planned on it, but it might be time." He shrugged. "The rent on the building is low enough that it's tempting. Besides, I've talked to a few people and, well, there's a need for someone in town to take care of simple things like wills, deed transfers, and property line disputes." He glanced at her and chuckled. "You know, the exciting stuff."

She laughed. "Right, I'd forgotten that lawyers actually do more than just sue people."

He smiled and pulled her closer. God, it really felt good being held by him.

"So, will you sign the lease? Move in full-time with your parents?" she asked and felt him wince.

"No." She felt her heart sink. "I'm thinking of looking at what Rose and my cousin Jacob have available up in Hidden Cove. Then see if there's anything available to rent in town in the meantime. Conner and Kara's new home is almost done being built, so maybe the apartment above Patty's will open up."

"Kara says that it's a few months out still," Robin said. "You could always move in with me," she said, half joking.

She felt his arms tense around her, but then he relaxed and chuckled. "I thought you wanted to keep this on the down-low?"

"I do," she admitted as she tried to hide the anxiety. "Besides, I'm not really keen on giving up my privacy," she lied quickly. "I'd be far too busy to entertain you." She held her breath and heard a slight chuckle emanate from him.

"It doesn't take much to keep me busy," he replied. "But I wouldn't dream of exposing our little... secret." He placed a kiss just above her jawline. She relaxed back into his chest and watched as the seagulls floated overhead.

A passing thought jumped into her head.

"There's a room." She sat up a little. "It's not much, a storeroom that I haven't cleared out yet in the barn. I've been thinking of having it turned into another guest changing room of sorts. If you want, you're welcome to it."

"If I can't find anything else in town, I may take you up on that offer," he said as he shifted slightly. "We're coming into Pride." He nudged her over and stood up.

For the next few minutes, she helped him lower the sails and secure everything as he steered them back into the harbor.

When they'd left the docks, most of the slots had

been empty. Now, almost every single one was filled with boats of all different sizes.

"What do you say to heading to the Oar for dinner?" he asked suddenly.

She thought about being seen with George at his family restaurant and held in a slight groan.

"We can do pizza instead?" he asked after watching her struggle with the idea.

It wasn't that she was trying to hide being seen with him. After all, he'd been on babysitting duty and that had entailed being seen together around town for the past few months. But this was different somehow. Now that they'd been together, she was sure everyone in town would see it clearly written in her eyes.

The chance of running into some of his family at a restaurant owned and run by his family was fairly high. Besides, the pizzeria was a little more casual than the Golden Oar and, after today, she knew that she needed to keep things casual between them. If she wasn't careful, she could see herself losing her hold.

"Pizza sounds good," she said casually.

"Pizza it is then."

Half an hour later, they stepped into Baked and were completely surrounded by a large group of members from the Jordan clan.

It was nice being swallowed by friendship and not one of his family members seemed to think that it was strange that they had arrived together.

However, her sister pulled her aside before they could order their pizza and pinched her in the side.

"What's up? Why you are arriving with George?" Kara whispered.

"It's nothing," she said quickly, which caused Kara's eyebrows to shoot up.

"Right, I don't believe that for a second." Her sister's eyes narrowed. "You look... different." Kara's eyes ran over her face and her hair. "What did you do? Run here?"

"No, George took me sailing," she whispered as she glanced around the crowded room.

George had blended into his family and if no one had witnessed them arriving together, there would have been no proof that they'd actually been together at all.

"Sailing?" Kara's voice rose slightly.

"Shh." Robin grabbed her good arm and nudged her a few steps away. "It's nothing. He just happened to mention last night at the event that he was going out today and I asked to tag along. I've never been sailing and thought it would be fun." She added a slight shrug to seal the story. "It was nothing. We just got back and decided to have a pizza." She sighed. "Now, can I go order?"

"You went on a date with George?" Her sister held her in place. "A full-day date?"

"Ugh," Robin groaned. "This is why I didn't tell you. I knew you'd make it into something it isn't."

"Why are you so determined to make it nothing?" Kara countered with a smile.

"Because George is... well, George." She lowered her voice. "We both know how he is with women. What he is," she added with a wave of her hand.

"What am I?" George's voice came from directly behind her, causing them both to jump slightly.

Two things happened quickly. First, her sister disappeared and second, the entire pizzeria grew so quiet, she could have heard a pin drop.

He watched Robin's eyes move around the dining room and waited for her answer. He had been a little surprised to see his all his cousins at Baked when they'd arrived a few moments earlier. Still, it wasn't uncommon for the family to have an impromptu get-together.

He'd been pulled in one direction while Robin had been pulled in another.

He hadn't needed to explain to his family why he was hanging around Robin. After all, they all knew that he was still officially on babysitting duty. He knew that everyone probably assumed they had just come from the venue to grab some food.

But when he'd hunted her down to see what kind of pizza she wanted to order, he'd overheard her last words to her sister and felt the sting of them.

It wasn't as if he had to defend himself to anyone, and he knew that Robin was probably just trying to keep their relationship under wraps. But after hearing her talking to

Kara, he wondered if there was a different reason Robin wanted to keep what was between them a secret.

He'd believed they'd had a perfect day together, but if Robin was playing him, well, it was better he found out now rather than later.

"It's just..." Robin said, glancing around before raising her voice slightly, "everyone in town knows how all the Jordan men are."

Several of those Jordan men behind him piped in.

"Handsome?" Matthew called out as he held his daughter in his arms.

"Rugged?" This from Jacob as he flexed his biceps.

"Hot as hell?" Conner added with a wink to Kara.

George stopped himself from rolling his eyes and turned to see Robin's response. She smiled slightly and he waited.

"Gigolos," she replied back with a chuckle, "each and every one of you."

The entire dining hall burst into laughter and conversation and voices filled the space once more.

Taking Robin's arm, he led them towards the front door. All joking aside, he wanted, no, needed to know what she'd meant.

"Do we have a problem?" he asked once they stood under the awning out front. The streetlights had flickered on and were now highlighting the light drizzle that washed over the town.

How often had he missed being in Pride? When he'd been at Berkeley, he'd missed the quiet of small-town life. Missed knowing almost everyone that passed by him, the sights and sounds of country life. But he'd also enjoyed the busyness of college life and figured each had their place in his heart. Now, however, he didn't think he could stand going back to the city life in Portland. Not when he'd had a glimpse of everything he could have here.

The possibility of having the future he wanted, the one he never believed he could dream of, here, in the small town he'd grown up in, the same town he'd dreamed of leaving behind, slightly scared him.

"Problem?" she asked, with a slight shake of her head. "No, I was just..." She took a deep breath, then quickly crossed her arms over her chest. He realized instantly that she'd already removed her coat inside and now stood in the chilly night in the sweater she'd changed into before they had left the docks. "Listen, we both know that I was trying to defuse the situation. I didn't mean anything by..." She shook her head and hugged herself even more.

Sighing with frustration, he realized that their conversation would have to wait. Not only was every eye in the pizzeria looking at them through the large front windows, but he was forcing her to stand out in the cold so he could stroke his ego and find out what she thought of him.

"Later," he said with slight frustration. "We can talk about this later." He moved over and opened the front door. She slowly walked towards him.

"George, I—"

"What kind of pizza do you want?" he interrupted.

Her eyes met his, and he saw her shoulders slump. "Whatever you order is fine."

"Beer?" he asked.

"Yes, please," she said stepping back inside. "Thank you."

The rest of the evening he kept to himself. He sat back and listened to his family chatter while he tried to keep his mind off of what Robin had meant.

Just exactly what was he?

What had she really meant? He hadn't heard much of the conversation before he'd interrupted the sisters.

By the time everyone started heading home for the evening, he had worked himself into exhaustion and was fighting off a headache.

"I'll drive you back home," he said to Robin.

"Don't bother." She motioned to her sister. "Kara and Conner have agreed to drop me off."

He wanted another moment alone with her but knew by the look on her face that she was done talking to him for the evening.

"Thank you for today," she said in a clipped voice.

"Any time," he replied. She slipped on her coat and disappeared out the front door with her sister and his cousin.

"What's eating you, cuz," Jacob asked as he slapped George on the back.

"Nothing." He tried to shake his foul mood off. "I was thinking of stopping in and talking to you and Rose." He motioned to their longtime friend as she stood laughing and talking to his sister Lilly. "I've been thinking of looking at those homes you two are working so hard at building up there on the hill. Maybe look at a place for me. You know, see if there's something there I'd like."

Jacob's eyebrows shot up. "Oh? So you're thinking of sticking around town this time?"

"Maybe. I've talked to Kathy about renting the place next to Suzie's shop," he admitted.

A slow smile crossed Jacob's face. "So there is something more between you and Robin? Is that why you want to stick around?"

"What?" He shook his head and started to deny it but figured he'd change tactics. "I've been talking to Uncle Todd, and he's pretty sure that Thomas Carson is going to continue to try and get under our skin. If he chooses to do that through legal channels, he thinks it would be best if we had a lawyer in the family close by."

Jacob nodded and then slapped him again on his back. "Good thinking. Swing by anytime you want. We're always up on the job site."

"I'll do that," he agreed, content that he'd steered his cousin away from the topic of Robin and their relationship. "So have you two set a date yet?" he joked as he motioned to Rose. Everyone in town knew that they were dating, and after the history they shared with one another, that was shocking enough. He knew it was just a matter of time before his cousin popped the question.

Jacob smiled, showing George his teeth. "I hear Conner and Kara have set a date." He nodded to the door they had just left out of.

"Yeah, I hear they're planning on getting married in a barn," he joked.

"It is a good place. Nice and romantic. Kind of like enjoying a full day of sailing," Jacob said with a smirk.

George set down his half-empty beer. "Well, on that note, I'm going to head home. It's been a long day."

He hadn't realized just how utterly exhausted he was until he climbed into bed. His body may have been tired, but his mind kept playing over the day's events.

How it had started out perfect and then turned so quickly once his family had gotten involved.

He thought about calling her. Texting her. Just to say he was sorry about... what? Reacting the way that he had. Then he realized he didn't believe he'd done anything wrong.

What had she been about to say? Oh, he knew of his reputation in town. How everyone believed he was a gigolo, as Robin had accused. Hell, most of the Jordan men had been accused of such before they'd found the loves of their lives.

He'd always expected and known that someday he'd follow them over the cliffs of insanity, as his father jokingly called marriage. He'd always believed that some-day, later in life, say in his late thirties, he'd start looking for the one woman that he'd settled down with.

An image quickly flashed in his mind of Robin filling that role in his life. As soon as the thought crossed his mind, he shook it away.

He was only twenty-five. Nowhere near ready to settle down.

For the rest of the night, he tossed and turned as his mind reused to shut down. He was thankful that he no longer had a job to get him out of bed early in the morning.

When his bedroom light flashed on just after seven

the next morning and his sister rushed to jump on his bed, for a split second, he believed he was back in school. He half expected that when he opened his eyes, Lilly would have braids in her hair and braces on her teeth.

"Come on, Georgie, it's time to get up," Lilly was saying as she bounced up and down on the bed, causing the springs on the old mattress to squeak.

"Go away," he said when realization hit him. He tried to cover his head with his comforter, but she held it away from him.

"Nope, can't. I'm supposed to get you to come into the kitchen," she said, still bouncing.

"Won't all that bouncing hurt the baby?" he asked. He waited for his sister to cover her growing belly with her hands and smile, then quickly snagged the blanket from her and covered his face.

"No," she answered. "Don't make me bring out the big guns. Mom wants you in the kitchen for a family breakfast." She leaned closer to him and lowered her voice. "Something's up."

He tossed the blanket off his face and looked at his sister. "She called you?"

"First thing this morning." Lilly shrugged.

"Did she tell you what the meeting is about?" he asked, curious enough that he sat up.

"No, but so far it's just the five of us. Which means, it's for us only."

"Or for our ears first," he said, throwing his feet out of the bed and getting up.

Lilly still sat on the side of his bed, and he turned

towards her. "Out." He pointed to the door. "I'll get dressed and be out in a minute."

Five minutes later, when he stepped into the kitchen, his mother was busy setting a large plate of pancakes on the dining table while his father poured Corey, Lilly's husband, a cup of coffee.

"Want some?" his dad asked.

"Yeah." He walked over and took a cup and held it out. He could feel his father's eyes on him as he assessed him. George had grown up under the watchful eye of a father who was the town's doctor. Which meant he had never had to worry about staying sick for too long. The flip side was that he was unable to hide anything from his parents. If he'd stayed up all night playing video games or had a few sips of beer or experimented with weed, his father had seen right through his lies.

"Rough night?" his dad asked him as he filled his cup.

"Couldn't shut down." He tapped on the side of his head.

"Does it have anything to do with why your mother called a family meeting?" his dad asked.

As an answer, he shrugged and sat down at the table.

"Okay, Mom," Lilly piped in after taking a couple pancakes and moving them to her plate. "What's this all about?"

His mother sat down at the end of the table and took a sip of her coffee while she waited for his dad to sit down.

"I had a chat with my brother earlier this morning," she began. "He's had a call from C & C Investments."

"Thomas Carson?" George asked.

"No, someone else from his legal offices." She pulled out a piece of paper from her pocket and scanned it. "A Patrick Banks."

"And?" George asked, wide awake now. "What are they trying now?"

"They want to have a meeting with Todd and his lawyers," she answered with a slight shrug. "Your uncle was hoping that you'd attend the meeting, since Josh Scott is in court today and can't make it. I think, somehow, they knew our lawyer was going to be out of town." His mother shook her head.

"What time?" George asked, wondering if he had time to shower.

"One," his mother answered quickly. "But Todd asked that you arrive a little earlier to go over a few things."

"As soon as I've showered, I'll head down to the office." He took another bite of his breakfast. Even though his mother wasn't as good of a cook as his uncle Iian, he'd missed his mother's breakfasts.

"Why are we here then?" Lilly asked through a full mouth of food.

"Do I need a reason to see my soon-to-be grandson?" his mother answered with a smirk. "Besides, I know that sometimes it takes a little family support to be able to kick things into gear.

"Mom tells me you're thinking of renting the store near Suzie's? That you're thinking of staying around for good?" Lilly asked.

"Thinking about it," he admitted.

Lilly nudged her husband under the table. Corey shifted and then nodded.

"Well, if you need a more permanent place to live... My brother and I still own the little place we purchased when we moved into town. Parker has been fixing it up a little and has most of it ready to be rented out."

Instantly George understood why his sister and brother-in-law had been invited to breakfast. He thought about moving into the rental, having the freedom to come and go until he could figure out something more permanent.

"I'll take you up on that offer," he said to Corey. "How close is she to being done?"

"You might have to do your laundry somewhere else for a week, but she's move-in ready today, if you want," Corey answered.

He thought about calling Kathy and letting her know that he'd take the unit as well. Might as well jump in with both feet. That could wait, he thought, until after he helped his uncle out. Wait until he knew for sure if he had a future in Pride or if he needed to pack up and head back to the city. Alone.

CHAPTER NINE

For the next few days, Robin stayed so busy that she didn't have time to think about George. Okay, she thought about him. She wondered why Aiden was there for the next two events instead of George to play the role of security.

She'd heard through the town's gossip train that he was busy helping his uncle out with something. She'd hoped that he would call or text her.

But then she remembered what she'd said the last time she'd seen him, what he'd overheard her saying, and understood why he hadn't contacted her.

The moment the last party guest left, she was going to call him. No matter how nervous she felt. She owed him an apology. Period.

Three hours later, after the last guest had finally left, she finished helping the crew clean up and then stepped outside and pulled out her cell phone as she walked back to the cottage.

When she hit George's number, she was slightly

surprised to hear his phone ring directly ahead of her. Jumping slightly, she turned the corner of the cottage to see him sitting on her front porch, his feet propped up as he sipped a beer.

Stepping onto the porch, he held up a fresh beer and smiled.

"It looks like you could use one of these," he said easily.

Taking the beer from him, she sat down in the chair next to him and took a long sip, letting the cold drink soothe her raw throat. She had never imagined that running her own venue would force her to talk so much. The first few events she'd ended up hoarse for a few days after.

After a while, however, she'd grown used to it. Still, a cold beer after a long day felt just as wonderful as getting off her feet for the first time in hours did.

"You called?" he asked after a moment.

She turned slightly towards him. "I wanted to apologize." She grew a little frustrated when he just continued to watch her and wait. "I crossed the line the other night and, for that, I'm sorry."

"I'm curious." He leaned forward and rested his elbows on his knees. His eyes bored into hers. "What were you about to say?" It was her turn to wait silently and watch him. "We both know how he is with women. What he is." He repeated her words, and she winced at having them thrown back at her. "What am I, Robin?"

"Up until a few weeks ago, I could have easily answered that." She leaned back, toed off her low heels, and lifted her feet up to rest on the old coffee table she'd dragged out to the porch. "Now..." She shook her head and thought about it. Then she turned her head and glanced at him. "I think we can both admit that you've had a revolving door of women." She held up her hand to stop him from interrupting. "Not that it's any of my business, just as long as while we're enjoying each other's company, it stays between us." He nodded quickly. "I suppose I listened to the town's gossip too much. It's been going around for as long as I've been here that you were a love-em-and-leave-em kind of guy. The kind of man my mother warned me and my sister away from." On this, his smile grew.

"And yet, here we sit." He raised his beer.

She chuckled. "I blame the sex hiatus I was on." She took another sip of her beer. "And those"—she motioned to his eyes— "sultry bedroom eyes."

He chuckled. "I've been accused of many things, but having sultry bedroom eyes has never been one of them."

"Don't get me started on your body and that six-pack," she warned with a smile. She sighed and let the smile fall away. "I misspoke and hurt you. For that, I truly am sorry."

He leaned closer and took her free hand in his. She hoped that meant that he'd forgiven her. That he was ready to move on from the entire ordeal. "I signed the lease on the unit next to the flower shop."

She arched her eyebrows. "You did?" What did that mean? Was he trying to tell her that he wanted to take their relationship—is that what this was called—to the next level? "That's... good. Right?"

He chuckled. "Yeah, my family seems to think so. My

brother-in-law has even rented me his old place in town. It's just a few blocks from here."

She glanced around and realized that his car wasn't in the driveway. "You walked over?"

"I did. After spending the entire day quitting my job and moving my things from Portland." He sighed heavily. "Which is why I needed the beer." He reached over and took the bottle and sipped again.

She understood now why he'd been missing. He'd been moving back to Pride.

"Are you all done?" she asked. "Moving in?"

"The house? Yes. I didn't have a lot of personal things to move. The business? No. Parker's going to get started in there tomorrow. Fresh paint, a few fixes..." He shrugged. "I'll have to purchase some office equipment and furniture. I was planning on heading into Edgeview tomorrow to start looking." He glanced sideways at her. "On a side note, I talked with your sister and found out that your event for tomorrow was cancelled."

"Yes." She smiled. "The birthday boy, Roy McCoy, is in the hospital with pneumonia." She leaned closer to him.

"Well, that does happen when you're... what? One hundred?" he said with a shrug.

"He is going to be one hundred and one," she supplied. "They've moved the party to next week. He's expected to make a full recovery."

When he let out another sigh and glanced off into the darkness, she followed his gaze and saw a jolt of lightning light up the sky over the dark waters.

"Since I was being lazy and didn't finish setting up

my bed..." His eyes turned back to hers, and she swore she felt her entire body vibrate at his gaze. "I was hoping you'd invite me in."

Smiling, she set her beer aside, then reached over and took the empty bottle out of his hands and set it next to hers. Then, with a slight tug, she had him following her inside without a single word.

His hands went to her hips the moment they stepped inside her bedroom. He turned her and covered her mouth with his, and she sighed and relaxed into his touch. Into him.

She'd believed she'd screwed this up. Believed he wouldn't come back to her. And it had hurt. She didn't want to admit it, but it had. She figured she'd think about what that meant later. For now, she was going to enjoy being with George. Enjoy feeling his strong hands roam over her skin, pleasing her.

It was as if he knew exactly what she wanted. What she needed. The more he touched her, kissed her, satisfied her, the more she wanted.

Later, when she fell asleep, wrapped in his arms, her head held tight against his chest, she thought over his words. What it meant to her that he was going to stay in Pride. What it meant to him and to his family. Everyone knew that no Jordan—or in this case, Stevens—was ever truly alone in Pride. They were an all-for-one-and-one-for-all kind of family.

She doubted that George could live the carefree life that he'd grown accustomed to in the city in such a small town. Facts were facts. There wasn't a revolving door of people to date in Pride. She knew that firsthand, having gone out on zero dates since moving into town.

Sure, there were a handful of potentials, but with fewer than ten thousand people living in a thirty-mile radius, you knew every single person and their history.

She knew that in the coming days, she was going to have to walk carefully to keep her reputation, and moreover, her heart, protected.

There was no doubt in her mind that she was just a distraction to George. After all, his history proved that he wasn't the settling-down type.

They may have known one another in passing for years, but that didn't mean they knew everything about each other.

That thought drifted with her for the rest of the night until she felt strong hands start to slowly circle on her skin.

Moaning and arching into the touch, she opened her eyes and saw George smiling down at her.

"Morning," he said softly as his hands continued to trace shapes over her skin.

"Morning." She smiled back at him and reached up to pull him down to her. She had a moment to worry about morning breath, but then he was kissing her and every worry, every fear fell away.

She couldn't remember spending a more perfect morning in her life. Taking a very slow and long shower with George was one of the highlights of her year. She didn't think the day could get any better, but then she sat in her small kitchen and watched him make breakfast for her.

He had insisted that she sit and enjoy a cup of coffee, and she'd taken him up on the offer. She couldn't think of a more relaxing way to start a day. Just knowing they were going to be spending the entire day together had her heart doing little flutters and jumps in her chest.

They took the breakfast out to the front porch and enjoyed the cool air coming off the water while they talked about what furnishings he needed for his office and home. The late evening's rain had washed everything, making it all seem cleaner, newer, fresher. Even the air smelled better after a rain.

The drive into Edgeview seemed shorter than normal. Maybe it was because he'd kept her so entertained with his story about how he and his cousins had conned his cousin Jacob into believing that bigfoot was real years ago.

"You really dressed up a dummy as bigfoot?" she asked as he pulled into the parking lot of the first furniture store.

He chuckled. "No, but we put our great-grandmother's fur coat on it. In the right light, it did the job of scaring the piss out of Jacob." He glanced over at her as he shut off the engine. "Hey, we had years of payback piled up. Do you know how many pranks he's played on the rest of us over the years?" he said with a smile.

It must have been wonderful to grow up in a family where the family lines blurred so much. The way he talked about his cousins was how most people talked about their siblings.

She and Kara were as close as sisters could get

without being twins. Even though they weren't twins, people often mistook them for each other.

She loved shopping, really did, and picking out furniture for a law office was no exception. When she found a classic solid maple desk and matching file cabinet, she pointed them out to George and was slightly surprised when he immediately agreed that they would work perfectly. She stood back while he arranged for them to be delivered later that week to his new offices, along with several other items they'd picked out already.

"With these," he said as the climbed back into his car and started it, "I just need another file cabinet, some office chairs, and some furniture for the waiting area."

For this, she suggested they head to another store across town, one she'd used herself when she got some of the stuff that she'd put in the guest changing rooms upstairs.

"How about lunch first?" he suggested. "I could use a burger and some greasy fries."

"Add a milkshake to that list and I'm in," she joked.

They enjoyed their greasy lunch at a place she expected he'd been to several times before since he walked in knowing exactly what he wanted.

It took her a little longer to decide what she wanted, but in the end, she doubled his order since she figured he knew what was good.

"I don't get into Edgeview as often as I had hoped," she admitted as they started eating. "A few shopping trips with my sister, but outside of that." She shrugged and glanced out the window as a light rain started falling outside.

"I know that look." He motioned with a fry. "That's the look of someone who misses the city life."

She chuckled. "Sometimes I do," she admitted. "You? You've only been back for a few months, but don't you worry that you'll miss it?"

She watched him closely for his reply.

"I guess I'll find out soon. I mean, I did grow up in Pride," he answered with a slight shrug.

"Yes, but were you the type of kid who always dreamed about escaping the mundane life in a small town? Or did you always dream of opening your own business and settling down here one day?" she asked.

"Both," he said easily. "At times, I couldn't wait to head to college." He finished off his burger and took a sip of his milkshake. "Mainly because I'd grown bored with everything that they tossed at me in school here. I'm somewhat of an overachiever in that area."

"Me too," she said with a smile and pointed with her thumb to her chest. "Valedictorian."

"Same." He smiled. "So, I headed off to Berkeley. Filled my brain with as much as I could, dated anyone I wanted." He shrugged slightly. "And dreamed of returning home someday."

Her heart quite literally jumped in her chest. She'd been under the assumption that he'd wanted to leave since the moment he'd been summoned by his uncle.

Maybe, if she'd been off about this small detail, there were other things about George that she'd been wrong about.

CHAPTER TEN

It didn't take long after the shopping day trip with Robin to get his entire office set up, with the help of his mother and his aunts, Megan and Allison. Robin wanted to help but was too busy with work and only had a chance to swing by after his family had disappeared to see the finished product.

"This is amazing," Robin said, running her fingers over the desk. "It fits perfectly in here. As do the two chairs." She motioned to the high-backed leather chairs she'd helped him pick out. They sat directly across from his desk for clients to relax in during consultations. One of his aunt's paintings hung on the freshly painted wall behind his desk, just above the low file cabinet that held a new printer/scanner combo machine that Josh had set up for his office and the receptionist area. He'd chosen to go with a laptop for him so he could take his work home some nights, and a desktop computer for the receptionist.

He had helped Parker paint all of the walls a slate blue, except for the conference room. There they had used a warm gray since the bookshelves took up most of the space and he wanted to lighten the space up some.

Parker had talked him into using a gray tile on the floors that looked like wood planks. His aunt and mother had chosen several paintings to hang throughout the space, with one of the *Dawn-Treader II* hanging behind his own desk along with his degree certificates, his state license, and his official town of Pride business license.

Instead of purchasing a desk for the receptionist, he'd opted to have Parker make a built-in unit. The custom desk made a large L shape and took up the entire left side of the reception area. There was a low table in the back that held the printer and housed the locked file cabinets underneath that would eventually hold all of his client's paperwork.

Across from the desk sat the new leather sofa and chair and the glass coffee table he'd purchased. His mother had supplied some magazines for the waiting area.

"Every reception area needs magazines," she'd said and organized a handful of them on the space.

It was the little things he hadn't thought of but that his mother and aunts had that made the space feel like something more than just an office. As he looked around, he realized that it felt as much like home as the place he was renting from Corey and Carter did.

Not that he was completely settled into the two-bedroom rental, but he was comfortable enough that Robin had spent a few nights there with him now. Since it was less than two blocks from her own place, he figured he could keep their privacy by just walking over to her place whenever he wanted.

"They're delivering the conference room table and chairs tomorrow," he said when she glanced across the hallway to the empty room. Most of the bookshelves that Parker had finished building in there were still empty. Boxes and boxes of books he had yet to unpack were stacked against the conference walls. He knew he had to unpack them all before they arrived with the table and chairs, but he figured he'd do it in the morning since he wanted to spend this time with her.

"Do you have enough books to fill those?" She walked across the space to look at the bookshelves.

He had to pry his eyes away from her tight butt, since she'd worn a pair of black leggings that clung to her curves. The soft silver sweater she wore over it stopped just below her waist and he noted that she had a pair of matching silver snow boots that went with the sweater.

Her long dark hair had been curled in soft ringlets, and his hands itched to feel their softness. Actually, his mind kept jumping to what she was wearing under those leggings. Was she wearing anything? Would he find her completely bare under the sweater as well?

"Yes. Law books, but yes. I have my personal collection still in boxes at home." He kicked one of the book boxes. "But there's enough in here to do the trick. I think."

Her eyebrows shot up. "Need any help?"

He hadn't wanted to take up any of her time. Not when he wanted to spend what little time they had together getting her naked and enjoying her.

"I couldn't ask..." he started, only to watch her bend over and open a box. His eyes once again went to her tight rear.

"Is there some sort of order?" she asked, and he felt his dick jump in his pants. "Or do you just want to stick them anywhere?" She glanced up at him.

He moved over to her and, without fully thinking about it, ran his hands over her hips until she straightened up. Then he pulled her close and covered her lips with his.

"You taste like spring." He sighed against her skin. "Did you wear this outfit for me?" he asked, running his hands down until he cupped her bottom and squeezed lightly. When she moaned, he smiled.

"What?" she asked with a shake of her head, which sent those curls bouncing around her shoulders.

Reaching up, he cupped her face and met her eyes.

"I wonder, if I looked," he said as his hand crept up under the sweater, "what would I find you wearing under this?" His fingers inched up higher, traveling over her ribs. He heard and felt her suck in her breath as her eyes closed and her head lolled back slightly. "Did you come here to torture me?" he asked softly as he continued to move up until he found her, just her, under the sweater. "Witch," he accused her as he cupped her breast and felt her nipple pucker for him.

A smile curved her lips as her arms wrapped around him.

"I've been accused of being lots of things. A witch isn't one them," she said as she buried her fingers into his hair.

"You didn't come here to help me unpack my books," he accused her as he moved her back a few steps until her shoulders were pinned against the new bookcases.

"I didn't?" she asked, meeting his eyes as his hands quickly moved lower. "Then why did I come here?"

For an answer, he quickly snaked his hand under the leggings and found her, just her, wet, ready for him, under the soft material.

"This," he growled next to her ear as he slid his fingers into her heat. "You wanted this." He nibbled on the skin just under her earlobe. "And me," he said, pushing his erection, still covered by his jeans, against her hips.

Her fingers tightened in his hair as she started trailing her mouth over his jawline.

"Maybe I did," she said, wrapping a leg around his hip, trying to pull him closer. "There's no law against it," she challenged and he smiled.

"How do you know?" He leaned back and looked into her eyes, seeing them go unfocused when he continued to move his fingers in and out of her, slowly now. "Are you a lawyer?"

He watched her shake her head from side to side, sending those long flowing curls moving again.

"No, but I know a really good one." She gripped his head and pulled his mouth back to hers.

He had meant to go slow, to enjoy himself, but the more she demanded from him, the more he knew he'd give her.

"Please," she said as she reached for the zipper of his jeans, "take me. Here. Now. Like this."

When she freed him, his fingers moved quickly to tug those sexy black leggings down her hips.

"My boots," she said with a soft chuckle.

He realized her leggings were pooled at her ankles, around her snow boots, and smiled.

"Here," he said, moving her slightly until he'd pinned her between the wall and his own body, lifting her slightly. "You can keep them on." He kissed her deeply as he stepped between her tangled legs. He sheathed himself with a rubber before nudging her thighs wider and sliding into her.

Her nails dug into his shoulders as he moved quickly. Their heavy panting almost echoed in the empty room. Her soft moans encouraged him to move faster, deeper, just move.

For a split second, when he felt her tighten around him, he had the realization that it had never been like this before. No woman had ever made him feel so... much.

An hour later, when they were surrounded by law books and half-empty Chinese take-out containers, he had a moment to think about just what that meant to him.

Robin was the kind of woman that could, after having what she described as knock-your-boots-off sex, turn to unpacking and sorting law books with him. No other woman he'd ever dated would have even touched a law book, let alone listened to him explain their differences and how to best organize them on the bookshelves.

Part of him wanted to share the joy of being in what he thought of as his first real relationship. But his knowledge that she wanted to keep things light between them outweighed his excitement. Outweighed even his own emotions for Robin. It was like a dark cloud over an otherwise sunny afternoon, the idea that his feelings were the only ones between the two of them. How did she feel about him?

"You never did tell me how the meeting between your uncle and Thomas Carson's lawyer went?" she asked from her spot on the floor surrounded by books.

"It didn't. Well, I suppose there was a brief meeting. The entire thing took less than five minutes. It was nothing more than an introduction of sorts." He shrugged and turned to place the next book in its place on the shelf. "Patrick Banks was so young and inexperienced; I doubt the ink on his state license was dry yet." He shook his head.

She peered up at him. "Remind me how long you've had yours?" she asked with a smile.

His eyes narrowed as he pointed at her with the next book. "I, at least, have almost a full year's experience working as a junior lawyer at a prestigious firm in Portland. Something tells me this is Banks's first job after graduation. One it was obvious he was ill prepared for."

"What happened?" She set down the stack of books she'd been holding on her lap and looked at him.

"The man almost fainted." He bent down to take the stack she'd just finished organizing.

"Seriously?" She gasped slightly.

"Well, no, but he definitely appeared as if he was going to get sick," he said with a chuckle. "It was almost as if..." He dropped off as he stared at the empty bookshelves.

Could Banks's meeting have been a ruse? A distraction? To what end? Why would Thomas Carson even hire someone so green? Let alone have him schedule a meeting. Was it to get the man's foot in the door?

He thought about every angle of the meeting. How the skinny young man, who had dressed in an ill-fitted suit, had shook for pretty much the entire meeting. Not to mention how out of place he'd looked in the offices of Jordan Shipping. There wasn't one employee that had worn a suit or a tie in the entire history of the building.

"George?" Robin asked, shaking him out of his thoughts. "You were saying?" She motioned to him.

Leaning his hip against the bookshelves, he sighed. "I just can't find the angle. I mean, why set a meeting in the first place if you're not going to talk business."

"What did Mr. Banks have to say?" she asked.

"Basically, he introduced himself and claimed that the firm he worked for had been hired by Thomas Carson or C & C Investments to look into my uncle's purchase of the land."

"A threat?" Robin stood up and moved over to set another stack of books down next to the stack he'd just set down.

"I don't think so. If it was meant as such, I would think Carson would have hired someone more..."

"Intimidating?" she supplied.

He smiled. "Less green."

"What happens now?" she asked. "Do you think Carson has something else up his sleeve?"

"Men like Carson always have something up their sleeves." He reached over and took her hands in his, then pulled her closer. She smelled so good, looked like heaven, and felt—his hands moved up her arms slowly—like silk. His mind instantly jumped, as did his body, to wanting her again. "Enough talk of business." He bent his head down and kissed her. "We have yet to christen my office," he said between kisses.

Hearing her soft laughter had his body further reacting.

CHAPTER ELEVEN

Waking in George's arms somehow still excited her. Even though they had been together like this for two whole months.

Now that he was no longer playing babysitter for his uncle, she didn't get to see him as often around the barn as she used to. Still, on occasion, he would show up and walk around the grounds and meet with her after everyone had gone.

She was beginning to think that the booty calls were all she was worth. Not that she was complaining. She did enjoy George, more so than she had any other man she'd been with. Not just in the physical aspect but in the realm of friendship as well.

He was easy to like since he made her laugh more often than anyone else that she'd dated had. Not that she could call what was between them dating. She didn't quite know how to describe it. Maybe she *was* only worthy of a booty-call.

Whatever the case, George made it very clear to her

that the physical portion of their relationship was as pleasing to him as it was to her. So she tried to push the rest of how she felt about him to the back of her mind.

The entire town of Pride was buzzing about the completion of the first home in Hidden Cove, which happened to be her parents' home. She would be spending her entire two days off helping them pack, move, and then unpack again in their brand-new home.

What she hadn't expected was a plethora of Jordan men lending a hand. In the end, she and her parents and Kara had sat around most of the day directing the men instead of working themselves. Not that she complained. After all, watching one Jordan man work was a delight; watching seven of them was heavenly.

She had to admit, she'd been sneaking onto the site on Lookout Lane since her parents had signed the contract. Watching the home going up made her feel somehow more connected to it.

She had spent months trying to figure out what the finished product would look like and, as she glanced around the home now, it didn't disappoint her. It wouldn't disappoint her parents either.

"Would you look at that view?" her mother said, stepping up behind her and wrapping her arm around Robin's waist. With a slight sigh, her mother turned to her. "And now I can see it every single day."

"It is pretty amazing," she agreed. "From up here, it's almost like you're looking down at a painting."

"Oh, we can still hear the waves." Her mother dropped her arm and walked over to open the sliding door, which let in the salt air and the soft sounds of waves crashing in the distance. "I had always believed that your father and I would be old and gray haired before we could afford to retire, let alone live in such a grand place."

She watched her mother turn a little circle in the dining room as she hugged herself. When she stopped, she turned back to her.

"This is the perfect home for grandchildren." Her mother's eyes narrowed.

Robin swallowed and then pointed across the room to where Kara was flirting with Conner.

"Don't look at me. They're the ones engaged." She felt her face heat as her heart sank slightly.

Her mother's smile grew as she moved over and once again wrapped her arms around her. "A mother can hope that both of her daughters will provide her with grand-kids. One day."

"Food's here," someone shouted out from somewhere inside the house.

"That will be the pizzas and beer your father and George went to go grab," her mother said, scurrying off to play hostess.

Just the thought of her father alone with George had her cringing. What did the two men talk about? Did her father know about their... arrangement?

Her eyes scanned the crowded room and found George in the kitchen. He was setting down a case of beer on the bar top.

He looked relaxed. As if he was enjoying himself. Not at all like a man who had been given the third degree from a concerned father, which had her relaxing instantly.

She'd overheard the story of how her father had had the talk with Conner when it was discovered that he and Kara were seeing one another. When the rumors had spread about their relationship, everyone in town had known that they were serious.

There was nothing serious about her and George. Well, except for the passion they shared with one another.

It wasn't as if she didn't dream about more with him. After all, he was... well, everything she'd ever dreamed of having in a man. Not only was he one of the most handsome men she'd dated, he was the kindest, most lighthearted, intelligent, sexy man she'd ever known. He always seemed to bring out the best in her, no matter the situation.

When she remembered the day that he'd taken her out sailing, it felt like a dream. A perfect dream. One that she doubted he or anyone else could ever top.

He'd mentioned taking her out again soon, but she knew he was very busy with his new business.

"You're quiet," her sister said, sitting next to her on the steps of the back porch, a plate of pizza balanced in her lap as she set down a can of soda.

"Just tired, I suppose," she lied. "Last night, the last guests didn't leave until after one." That much was true. What she didn't tell her sister is that George had come over, and they'd spent the rest of the night entertaining one another.

"I'm hoping Mom will start allowing me to lift more than two pounds after tomorrow." She motioned to her left arm. "Then I can come back full-time and help out." Her sister sighed. "I've missed it."

"You shouldn't push yourself. Remember, you were shot." When she thought about how close she'd come to losing her sister, her stomach turned. Setting her half-eaten pizza down, she tucked her knees up to her chest and looked out at the view.

"It's been almost three months." Kara rolled her eyes. "I've almost got full range of motion back and"—she leaned closer and lowered her voice— "I've been working my left arm." She lifted her arm and flexed as if showing off her muscles.

"Does Mom know?" she asked quickly, glancing around and looking for their mother, who happened to be Kara's physical therapist.

"No, and don't you tell her. I've gotten to where I can do three reps with five-pound weights." Kara smiled. "That's a huge improvement."

Robin's stomach did a little turn. There had been a point when her sister couldn't even lift her arm. Now, with it still in a sling tucked by her side, Robin wondered if her sister would ever make a complete recovery from the bullet that had torn through her life.

She wrapped her arm around her sister's shoulder and hugged her lightly.

"You're going to be back to your old self in no time, just don't rush it. I can handle things until you're ready," she assured her.

"But you shouldn't have to do it all alone," Kara replied with a frown. "This was our adventure."

"And it still is. You're there every event, helping me organize, coordinate. If I needed something lifted"—she glanced around and spotted George walking towards them and raised her voice slightly— "I'd hire a Jordan. After all, they've killed it today with moving our parents' stuff."

George stopped directly in front of them and smiled. "My great-grandfather should have started a moving company as well as a shipping company."

Kara and Robin chuckled.

"I'm going to go find my fiancé," Kara said suddenly, standing up. "Thank you for all of your help today," Kara said, touching George's shoulder with her right hand as she passed him.

"Any time. I hear you and my cousin will be moving into your place next week." George leaned closer. "It's a good thing I'll be in Portland then."

Kara smiled. "I hear the rest of your family has already signed up to lend a hand. I think we can make do with one less Jordan man."

"You'll find out soon enough, I'm the strongest Jordan there is." George flexed his biceps, and Kara laughed as she walked away.

Robin thought quickly of how easy he melded into her family. How well all the Jordans got along with her family, actually.

Which had her thinking about what was going to happen when they called things off. Could they still be friends or even friendly, for that matter?

George sat down next to her and picked up the rest of the slice of pizza she'd discarded and started finishing it off.

"So," he said between bites, "pretty amazing view, huh?" He motioned to the colorful sunset across the small backyard of her parents' new home.

"Amazing." She sighed. "It's funny, I thought the sunsets from the cabin were gorgeous, but from up here..." She hugged her knees to her chest again and let out a soft sigh. "It's spectacular."

"I'll be enjoying it soon myself," he said after taking the last bite of crust.

"You will?" she asked, glancing at him sideways.

"I signed the paperwork yesterday. I'm three lots up." He motioned to the right. "Lot three," he said with a smile. "Same view, just a little up the hill from here."

"Congrats," she said. He'd mentioned several times how he was looking at having a home built up here, along with the rest of his cousins. But this news somehow made it a little more real. And for some reason, that made her stomach uneasy.

"You're heading out of town?" she asked, remembering his words to her sister.

"Yeah, court date next week in Portland, and I still have a few things in storage that need to be moved down here." He leaned back against the stairs. His eyes rested on her instead of the soft pink and purple hues of the sky.

She felt a little self-conscious since the rest of his family and hers were just inside the house, steps away.

"How long will you be gone?" she asked, only expecting to make small talk.

Instead of answering right away, he leaned closer and whispered, "Going to miss me?"

The huskiness of his voice sent bumps rising all over her skin.

"No," she said automatically. But the truth was, she *was* going to miss him. At first, when Kara had moved out of the cottage, she'd enjoyed her privacy, her alone time. Now, however, she'd gotten used to having George around, filling her time.

Whatever was she going to do with her free time after he'd had his fill of her? Could she ever go back to being... alone? It was another reason she feared for the end of their arrangement.

"I'll only be gone two nights. Three tops." He tilted his head and ran his eyes over her. "I wish you could come with me," he said softly.

"I have..." She started to tell him about the massive Valentine's dance she was hosting for the high school that week but stopped when he held up his hand.

"I know, I looked at your schedule," he said with a sigh. "Still, it doesn't stop me from wishing." He moved slightly closer. "Dreaming about spending two nights alone with you in the city. Two days where we could do whatever we wanted. Go wherever without hiding from people we know." His hand brushed the back of hers, and she longed to turn her hand and grab hold of his.

Swallowing, she leaned away when she heard the back door slide open behind them.

"There you are, George," her mother said, causing him to quickly stand up. "I think we need your help moving my hutch into the dining room."

"At your service," George said. Before leaving, he gave her a quick nod.

What did it say that he wasn't even going to be around for Valentine's Day? The more she thought about it, the more she realized it was a telltale sign of what exactly their relationship was. A convenience and nothing more.

She took the next ten minutes to settle her heart as she watched the last lights of the colorful sunset sink below the horizon of the Pacific. The view would never get old.

But since it was mid-February, the chill of the night had her retreating inside to help her mother start to unpack boxes and boxes of dishes and kitchen items.

The following days, she tried to keep herself so busy that she wouldn't notice George's absence, let alone think about the hurt of rejection when Valentine's came and went without seeing him.

He did text her that evening, but she'd been so busy with the dance, she hadn't had time to respond until well past midnight.

"I know you're probably rustling up a few teenagers, but I wanted to let you know that I made it here okay. The city isn't any fun without you here to help me get into trouble. I'm off to eat some really good Indian food at a place my cousin swears is the best place in Oregon. Dinner alone in the city on V day. Just what I hoped tonight would be. Know that I'm thinking of you. Goodnight."

Okay, so that text made up for the lack of flowers or attention. After all, she'd reminded herself that if he'd gotten anything for her, he would have had to order it from his cousin Suzie's shop. And once his cousin knew he'd sent her flowers... their little secret would have been out.

At least that's what she had tried to convince herself of. She pushed the fact that there were flower shops in Edgeview that delivered to Pride to the back of her mind.

The day after Valentine's Day, the news of Jacob and Rose's engagement spread like wildfire everywhere throughout town. Robin got a little taste of what it would be like if her and George's relationship became public.

She was currently standing in the Golden Oar, waiting for her take-out order, and overheard no fewer than five different tables talking about the engagement. They weren't trying to hide the excitement, since the five tables were practically leaning across the empty space between them and chatting openly about it together. Indeed, the longer she stood there in the entryway of the restaurant, the more she came to realize the entire place was abuzz with the news.

"Did you hear?" Kara asked her when she walked into the back kitchen in the barn. Since it was just past noon, there wasn't a soul around except for the two of them. In less than two hours, the place would be buzzing with activity, preparing for another full event.

"Yes," she said, trying to hide the annoyance that came with a growing headache. "Jacob and Rose..." She waved her hand.

"What?" Kara stopped what she was doing and looked at her. "What about them?"

Setting down the bag of take-out, she looked across the way at her sister. "They're engaged." She shook her head. "What was your news?"

"They are?" Kara squealed. "How exciting."

Robin waited. "Your news?" she reminded her when her sister continued to remain quiet.

"Oh, it's not as exciting as your news. Roy McCoy has made a full recovery and is looking forward to his one-hundred-and-first birthday party this week." Kara smiled back at her.

CHAPTER TWELVE

Spending a few nights in the city would have never both-
ered him before. He would have simply hit a few bars
and, most likely, found someone willing to share his time
and his bed with.

Now, however, he found his time droning on and
ended up falling asleep watching an old movie in his
hotel room on Valentine's night.

He knew that Robin had a large high school dance to
tend to, which got him thinking about his own school
dances. They had never been hosted at a place as elegant
as the barn and had instead been held in the high school
gym. Dancing next to your school sweetheart with a hint
of sweaty socks and jocks in the air just had never been
something he'd looked forward to.

He bet that he would have looked forward to dancing
under the strings of lights in the romantic atmosphere he
knew Robin and Kara arranged for each dance.

The sisters had a knack for turning something
common into something... extraordinary. Just like she'd

taken their casual relationship and turned it into something deeper. He hadn't expected to feel as much for her as he did.

He supposed it was because they'd known one another casually all of their lives. Then again, he'd never really paid any attention to the sisters before, so he couldn't explain why it mattered now.

She mattered.

The drive back to Pride a few days later was mundane and tedious. He was thoroughly excited to get out of the city and wondered why he'd been thrilled to return to the craziness of the hustle and bustle.

He'd run into a few of his exes the night after Valentine's Day when he'd bumped into a friend who had strong-armed him into heading to a bar and having a few drinks.

It hadn't been hard to turn down his exes' advances, which had gotten him thinking and brooding so much that he'd been a downer and had left less than an hour after he'd arrived.

He continued to think about his and Robin's relationship as he grew closer to Pride. How had she gotten under his skin so quickly? Part of his mind played the possibility that this had been her plan all along.

Had she trapped him? Trapped him into giving up everything he'd wanted in the city, to leave it all behind and tie himself down to small-town life. A life where, he knew all too well, he could be limited in every aspect.

Especially his career. Sure, he owned his own law practice. If you could call it that. He had more than a handful of new clients already, each of them needing small things like their wills updated or small disputes handled. Not that he didn't like the work or the people of Pride. Those, along with enjoying his time with Robin, were his only saving grace.

What did that say about him? Was he becoming too attached to her?

Moving into his own place had afforded him privacy, but he'd filled his free time with Robin, or he did when she was available herself.

He'd told himself that a few nights away from her would be good. After all, he'd have the time to think about their relationship and the importance of it. Now as he parked in front of the barn and watched her clearing the tables from the Sunday brunch, he realized that he'd screwed up.

The old proverb was true. Distance did make the heart grow fonder. Shit. He was in trouble.

He almost threw the car in reverse and high-tailed it out of there, but then her head snapped up, as if she'd felt his eyes roaming over her from the distance.

He watched that sexy smile of hers curve her lips up, causing the little dimples on the side of her mouth to flash. He actually felt his heart skip.

"Shit." He turned off the car and tried to settle back down as he crossed the distance to her. She set the table-cloth she'd finished folding back down and wrapped her arms around him.

"Hi," she said easily.

"Hi." He glanced around, hinting that they might be seen.

"My sister went home an hour ago," she said easily,

then she leaned up and brushed her lips against his. "I have a small dinner party later tonight, but we have a few hours until I have to start getting things ready." She started pulling him back towards the open barn door.

If it hadn't been for her urgency, he would have pulled away, come up with some excuse as to why he was needed elsewhere.

Her kisses drew him in, held him hostage, and he allowed her to pull him into one of the private changing rooms where he laid her out on a cream-colored settee. As he hiked up the skirt of her flowered spring dress, settled between her thighs, he knew that he'd passed that point. Now, if either of them called it off, he wouldn't be able to walk away unscathed.

Tasting her on his lips, he realized that he'd been starved the last few days. He felt her thighs wrap around his shoulders as he lapped at her, felt her growing desire as he pleased her. When her release came, he knew instantly that it was up to him to pull away.

If he was going to survive Robin Jenkins, he couldn't spare another moment, another tender kiss or sensual moment with her.

She held something that no other woman had ever held. His heart. Completely.

"What?" Robin asked when he stood looking down at her.

Her eyes were dreaming. The skirt of her dress hiked up to showcase her perfect thighs. Her silk panties were discarded on the floor.

Her cheeks were pink, heated from the release. Her

lips were swollen from either his kisses or from her nibbling on them.

Her long dark hair was fanned out over the settee, and he felt his entire body itch to consume hers, to enjoy all the different ways to please her.

Still, he took a step back.

"I..." He shook his head, trying to clear the thoughts of tossing their agreement aside and returning to her, here, now. Telling her how he felt. That he wanted more from her. Why not?

His feet moved back again as she reached up for him.

"George." His name was just a whisper.

"I..." he started again. "I have to..." He turned and fled. He'd like to think he hadn't run from the room like a scared man, but later that evening, when he was tossing and turning in bed, he realized it was the truth.

He'd texted her an apology. Claimed that he'd had to be somewhere, had a meeting or a client waiting for him. But the truth was he'd been a chicken. Completely and utterly.

He ran into her two days later at Sara's Nook. It stung a little when her smile was strained. He knew he owed her an explanation and an apology. Since she was sitting at a table with her sister and parents, he sat across the room from her and shot off a text to her.

"Do you have some free time today?"

He heard her phone chime with the received message and waited for her response.

"No, not until tomorrow."

"Breakfast? My place?" he responded.

"Lunch. Mine?" she responded back.

"I'll be there." He tucked his phone into his pocket as he finished his apple cinnamon fritter and coffee.

As he was walking out, he bumped into Josh Williams. The man owned and ran a fantastic online security firm and was married to Carrie Brogan, now Williams.

Josh had setup George's new computer systems for his office. Not that he'd had a lot of time to talk to the guy, since the man had come in after dark and set everything up at night.

"It's good that you're back in town for good," the man said, shaking George's hand easily. "You're just the man I was hoping to run into." He motioned to the door. "Have a moment?"

"I do," he answered after mentally confirming he had a free schedule. Following Josh inside, he waited as the man ordered a breakfast burrito and coffee, then sat across from him in a back booth.

He'd watched Robin and her family leave moments before he'd headed towards the door himself.

"So, what can I help you with?" he asked.

Josh sighed and shook his head. "You may have heard some of my... family's history."

"Your dad?"

"Yeah." He nodded.

"He's still locked up, right?" George asked.

Josh sighed. "He earned ten years after the manslaughter charges when he drove drunk and killed Mike Collins."

"How long ago was that?" George asked, already getting the idea of what Josh needed.

"Six years now. He's up for parole. The doctors are trying to get him out on medical release." Josh stopped and waited as his coffee was set in front of him, along with his breakfast.

"Want me to look into it further?" he asked.

"I'd appreciate it. Now that Carrie and I have Brian"—the man's face lit up when he talked about his son—"well, I need to ensure that what's mine is safe." His face dropped again.

"Say no more." He nodded. "If you can get me his case..."

Josh pulled out his phone, and George heard his phone chime.

"His case files," he said with a smile.

"Right," George nodded. "I'd forgotten how much of a tech genius you were."

Josh chuckled. "I'd come prepared. I saw you through the window. Carrie and I had talked about coming in to see you." He shrugged. "You saved us a trip."

"I'll let you know what I find." He started to get up.

"Actually, there's a little more to it," Josh said, setting down his mug.

"Okay." George leaned back. "Shoot."

"My uncle, my father's brother, Carl. He's been... pestering my mother over the past few months."

"I didn't know your dad had a brother." George tried to think back to all the stories he'd heard about Kevin Williams. All the problems he'd caused his family over the years.

"Carl was a lot younger than my dad. When my grandparents divorced, my grandmother took Carl to

California. My granddad, well, he kept my dad, and the rest is history." He shook his head. "Anyway, Carl is suing my mother."

"Why?" George leaned forward. He'd known and respected Brenda Williams his entire life. The woman, who was no doubt back in the kitchen in the bakery, baking her heart out, had been nothing but kind to anyone in town.

"Carl claims that my dad is due the land my mother inherited from my grandmother. My mom's mother. Apparently since my dad is in jail, he signed over his power of attorney to Carl." Josh shook his head. "I haven't had time to look into the guy, since I'd pretty much forgotten the man existed until I found the legal letter in my mother's things."

"Say no more." He waved Josh off again. "I'll look into both of these and let you know when I find something."

"Thanks." Josh seemed to relax for the first time. "I can't tell you how happy Carrie and I both are that you decided to come back to Pride and stay. I'm also in need of a good business lawyer." Josh's eyebrows rose slightly. "It's tiring working with my guys out of Portland. Think you can handle corporate legal issues?"

George laughed. "It's actually my specialty. Let me know what you need, and I'll get on it."

"Great, I'll have my people contact you, get you up to speed on what's going on. We have a few big contracts coming up that need going over." Josh reached out his hand. "I can't thank you enough."

George chuckled. "You can, when you get my bill."

Josh laughed. "Which reminds me, your mother said I should ask for the family rate."

George groaned. "Yeah, I'm giving everyone in Pride that rate," he said as he stood up. "Big families." He rolled his eyes.

By the end of the day, George was very thankful he'd bumped into Josh Williams that morning. Not only had Josh forwarded his father's case information and the file on his uncle and his mother, but his secretary had forwarded him a zip file filled with files related to Josh's company, Internal Security, and Carrie's business, Carrie's Sanctuary.

With just one short meeting, George's schedule and client list was now packed.

Once word got out that George was handling everything for Josh, his phone didn't stop ringing.

He'd actually had to call in his mother to help him answer the phones while he looked over Kevin William's case.

He knew from the stories of the man that if there was a possibility of Kevin getting out of prison soon, the town would have to be on alert. There were things George could do to ensure that the man served his full sentence, especially since the man's medical files had been transferred along with the rest of the legal files.

"Do you remember Mia Dylan?" his mother asked as she leaned against the door jamb of his office.

"Mia?" He glanced up from his computer screen. "Mia Dylan?" The name was familiar.

"She's an old friend." His mother waved her hand. "She used to work for Louis Breg. Anyway, she was his legal assistant and retired a few years back. She's been thinking of coming in and applying for a job. I think that after today"—she waved her hand as the phone rang again— "I'll leave you her number." She rushed back up to the front to answer the phone.

Moments later, Mia's contact information came through on his phone.

Since he had the time, he called the woman and talked to her quickly. She agreed to come in first thing in the morning, and he hung up and got back to work.

It wasn't until shortly past midnight when he'd finished looking over all of the contracts for Internet Security that he pulled out his cell phone and saw Robin's latest message cancelling their lunch date tomorrow.

CHAPTER THIRTEEN

Robin knew she was a coward. But after seeing George that morning at the bakery, seeing the way he avoided eye contact with her, she knew for a fact that things were over between them.

The hurt and pain she'd felt after he'd left her in the bride's changing room, sprawled out on the settee like a buffet he'd just enjoyed, had been so great. She'd held it together and had tried to busy herself to avoid having to wonder why he'd sprinted away from her.

The scared look he'd had in his eyes as he'd looked down at her had hurt more than any rejection she'd gotten in her past relationships.

Then again, she reminded herself that what had been between her and George wasn't really a relationship. What it had been was an arrangement, and it was now apparent to her that George was over it. Over her.

She realized that he'd allowed her to pull him into the room and he'd, no doubt, out of obligation, followed along with her desires.

That didn't mean that she had to go along with his. Which is why, shortly before she'd grown busy with the evening's event, she'd texted him and cancelled their lunch date for the following day.

She'd only checked her phone a few times during the event—okay, more than a dozen times—and each time, she'd been hurt even more when he hadn't responded.

It had been the cause of a restless night. The following morning, she had a brunch scheduled and dragged all the way through the event.

Her eyes stung, her chest hurt, and she felt like she wasn't going to be able to make it through the rest of the day.

She drowned herself with caffeine, hoping that the boost would be enough, but felt herself lagging as the lunch hour approached.

Since George hadn't responded to her message yet, she assumed he understood that she'd gotten the hint and knew that he wanted to take a step away.

"I'm going to head over and meet Conner for lunch at Baked. Do you want to tag along?" Kara asked her.

"No." She shook her head. "I think I'm going to finish up here and then head over to the cottage for a quick nap." She smiled. "Late night."

"Okay." Her sister waved to her as she left. "See you in an hour."

Robin finished cleaning up in the kitchen, placing the rest of the dishes in the dishwasher and drying off the countertops. They hadn't needed the kitchen staff for brunch, but she knew that Joy would be coming in soon for the event later that night, and if there was anything out of place in her kitchen, Robin wouldn't hear the end of it.

"Hiding from me?" A deep voice caused her to jump and drop the rag she'd been using. Spinning around, her eyes fell on George casually leaning against the opened door, watching her.

God, he was so handsome, it hurt just looking at him. He was wearing dark jeans and a button-up shirt with the sleeves rolled up to the elbows.

He'd recently gotten a haircut, something she'd noticed when he'd returned yesterday as she'd been grabbing his head while he'd...

She shook those thoughts from her mind and turned away from him.

"No," she lied.

"Then why cancel lunch?" he asked, and she could hear that he'd moved closer to her.

Instead of answering, she bent down and picked up the rag she'd dropped and tossed it into the hamper in the closet.

"I've got—"

"Don't say work. Because this place is empty,"

She turned on him. "Things to do. I'm far too behind in..." He waited, his eyebrows shooting up as he waited.

"Robin, take a walk with me?" He motioned to the doorway.

"No." She shook her head. She knew what was coming. Wanted to avoid it, avoid the pain that she knew would come with his rejection. "I needed to..." She stopped talking when his hand rested on her shoulders, and he pulled her back against his chest.

"I'm sorry about yesterday," he said softly. "Give me a chance to explain."

She closed her eyes and, for just a moment, swayed into his embrace. Relaxed for a split second.

"I can't," she said softly, already feeling the effects of him moving away from her when he turned her around and dropped his hands from her.

"I never meant for this... it's not like I planned..." He shook his head, and tears stung the back of her eyes.

"Just go," she said softly. She stood still and stiff. "We both agreed that this is what it would be. That we'd part as friends."

"Is that what you want?" he asked, his eyes scanning hers.

She wanted to shout *no* but instead remained quiet. He took a step away from her, then another.

"I hadn't planned... If I hurt you, I'm sorry," he said softly before turning and walking out.

She waited until she heard his car disappear out the gravel parking lot before her knees gave out on her. She buried her face in her hands and cried until there was nothing left in her.

Heading back to the cottage, she showered, stood under the hot water, and cried some more.

When her phone alarm chimed, she climbed out, dressed, and got ready for the dinner event. She pasted on her best smile and pulled it together so that no one would ever know that her heart was breaking into a million pieces.

That night, lying alone in her bed, she tried to convince herself that it was for the best. She'd known going into this that George wasn't the type to stick around. Hell, he'd only been there because his uncle had hired him to watch over her and her business.

She had been a job. Then she'd been a distraction. Entertainment. Just like he had been to her. Until he wasn't. Until things had changed. At least in her mind and her heart.

She'd been a fool to think that he'd felt the same way she had. That he'd grown to care for her as she cared for him.

Wasn't this how all of her relationships had gone? She'd felt too much. Too quickly. It was the number one reason women scared men away. Or so she figured. At least it was in her book.

The following morning she had free. Actually, her next event wasn't until eight that evening. Not wanting to be seen in town, she stuck to the cottage. She took a short walk along the beach, sitting in the wet sand as a light drizzle washed over everything, making it appear cleaner.

Just like her life. She was back to where she'd been months ago, before she'd taken George's hand and led him from this very spot. Alone.

She should have protected herself and her heart more. The slip into caring too much had been so slow that she hadn't realized it was happening until it was too late.

When Kara showed up to help set up for the next event, her sister instantly knew there was something wrong with her.

"What's wrong?" Kara rushed over to lay the back of her hand on Robin's forehead. "Are you sick?"

"No, just... tired." She shook her head. "I'll be fine," she replied, not wanting to make a big deal over how she was feeling. After all, her and George's relationship had been a secret. She couldn't very well cry on her sister's shoulder when Kara had no clue why.

"Why don't you go home, rest. I've got this. It's just a dozen guests. The kitchen staff can take care of most of the heavy lifting. I can call Conner over to help me out."

She thought about spending a night at home. Alone. Maybe even taking a long, hot bubble bath while she was at it.

"Are you sure?" she asked, rubbing a hand over her forehead. She hadn't realized she had been fighting off a headache until then.

"Here." Kara walked over, took one of the waiting plates of food, and handed it to her. "Go home, eat, rest. I'll call Conner and we'll clean and lock up afterward." Kara gave her a one-arm hug and then nudged her towards the door.

It was strange, being home before dark. Knowing she had the entire night to herself and that George wouldn't be making an appearance later to slip into her bed. That there would no longer be long lazy nights of pleasing one another or early morning showers and breakfasts together.

She was going to miss his friendship as much as she missed what he did to her body.

Sitting out on the front porch, she listened and watched the rain increase as she ate most of the dinner Joy had prepared for the guests.

When she was done, she took the plate inside,

stripped off her clothes, and climbed into a hot bath after tossing in a jasmine scented bath bomb. Piling her hair in a messy bun on top of her head, she slipped on her earbuds and listened to her favorite mix, making a point to skip past any song that had anything to do with breakups. Putting on one of the face masks she'd ordered online, she sank below the steamy, colored water and thoroughly enjoyed the relaxation.

At one point, she must have fallen asleep. When she opened her eyes, the light had shifted into full darkness. Since she hadn't turned on a light in the bathroom before climbing into the tub, it was pitch dark.

Letting the cool water out of the tub, she stood up and reached for a towel, searching the dark bathroom and hoping she didn't slip and fall in the process.

When her hand landed on the towel, she let out a sigh and then froze when she heard a floorboard outside the bathroom squeak. Her mind went completely blank. Her cell phone sat somewhere on the edge of the tub. If she tried to find it, it might slip into the still draining water. If she turned on the light, whoever was out there would know she was in the bathroom. If the sound of the draining water wasn't already a giveaway.

Quickly wrapping the towel around herself, she tiptoed over to the door and ensured that the lock was engaged. The light clicking sound as she flipped the button sounded to her like a shotgun in the darkness.

A scrape of footsteps sounded at the end of the hallway, and she knew that whoever it was had turned back towards the bathroom.

She picked up the first item she found, figuring she

would have to fight the assailant off and escape and run over to the barn in hopes that her sister and Conner were still around. She doubted it was that late.

Yanking open the door, she screamed loudly as she swung out and came inches from slamming George in the forehead with the toilet plunger.

"What the..." He held the end of the plunger inches from his head and looked at her in shock, just as the towel she'd wrapped around her slipped to the floor, leaving her completely naked.

George's look of horror turned to humor then to lust so quickly she didn't have time to blink.

Then he was laughing and pulling her into his arms.

"What are you doing here?" She tried to jerk out of his arms as he continued to laugh. "Let go of me," she said, still trying to break out of his hold.

"I talked to your sister," he said, still laughing. "she mentioned that you were sick so I came to check up on you. I called out and when you didn't answer"—he pulled back slightly and his smile slipped when his eyes met hers — "I let myself in with my key. The place was dark, and I thought you were sleeping. I was going to check up on you, make sure you were okay, and leave before you knew I was even here." He smiled again. "I had no intention of getting beamed by a plunger and getting a show while at it." His eyes moved down to the curve of her breasts, as they were still pushed up against his fully clothed chest.

"Let me go," she said, trying once again to break free.

"Naked hugs," he said a little breathless. "I think I deserve this after being attacked."

"You broke in here. Scared me. I thought..." She

shook her head and then stopped trying to break free from his hold. In truth, she knew there was no way to get free from him until he released her. "I fell asleep in the bath," she said as the last of the water left the tub with a sucking sound.

"I can smell that." He bent his head and sniffed her neck, sending goose bumps over her skin. Her knees buckled slightly as a wave of desire washed over her. "You smell like jasmine." He brushed his lips over her skin.

She didn't know if he'd done it intentionally, but it had the same effect on her system. She wanted him. Damn it.

CHAPTER FOURTEEN

George really had had no intention of doing anything other than checking up on a friend after talking with Kara. He'd wanted to let her know that he wouldn't be working that night and had sent over Conner instead. But the moment he'd seen Robin, everything had changed.

Kara had sounded worried about Robin and had explained how her sister had never been sick. Not once in the past year and a half.

Kara had practically begged him to come over and check up on Robin, since due to Robins absence, she'd need Conner's help and that they would be too busy with the event.

Getting flashed by Robin in the hallway had been the icing on the cake of a totally miserable day. He'd brooded, or so his mother and Mia had claimed.

The moment the woman had stepped in the office door, he'd remembered her. She'd been a longtime family friend. He couldn't believe that he hadn't placed her before seeing her. He supposed he'd been too busy yesterday to give it much thought. Besides, she'd moved to Edgeview when he'd been in middle school and hadn't returned until after he'd left for college.

Now, she and her husband were back in Pride, and she was looking to fill some of her free time after retirement.

Since she had worked as a legal assistant for more than thirty years, he'd hired her on the spot.

That day had been filled with even more calls, along with more than half a dozen people dropping by his office for a quick chat.

The way things were going, he was going to have to set regular hours and think about hiring more part-time work to help out.

He supposed it was a good thing, but at this point, he'd hoped for a quiet day where he could think about what had happened between he and Robin.

He'd been so busy that day that he hadn't even had a moment to himself.

He'd just finished a late-night dinner of cold pizza as he scoured over Josh's father's case when Kara had contacted him.

Now, with Robin's naked body pressed up against his, he realized his mistake. He hadn't given her the opportunity to change her mind about him.

What he needed to do was prove to her that there could be more between them. That she could grow to love him.

Everyone always said that if you loved something, you had to fight for it, which is exactly what he intended to do.

He couldn't believe that he had almost given up so easily. The miserable day he'd had proved to him that he didn't want to be without her. Not yet, at any rate.

He felt the soft skin of her lower back under his hands as he held her against him, and he saw desire flash quickly in her eyes. He knew that specific look from her. That was the look she got just before she attacked him. Only this time, she didn't move. Didn't even breath, it seemed. Was it too late?

"Let me go," Robin said again, this time without any emotion. He dropped his hold on her.

She quickly scooped up the towel at her feet, covered her body, and turned to go back into the bathroom.

He reached out quickly and laid a hand on her shoulder.

"Robin." His voice was slightly hoarse. Filled with desire for her. She must have sensed it because without glancing back, she sighed.

"I don't think I can keep doing this," she said. "I can't keep up with the games."

That was a good thing. Right? Was she struggling with wanting more between them as well?

Hope sprung up and he nudged her to turn back towards him.

When her chin remained dropped and her eyes wouldn't meet his, he gently nudged her chin up until her eyes met his. Seeing the tears undid him. He gathered her in his arms again, this time holding onto her to comfort her.

"What's wrong?" he asked into her hair.

"You," she said with a sigh. "You're here. I was...

prepared to let you go." His arms tightened slightly at this news. "How am I supposed to let you go?" She rested her forehead against his chest. "You don't play fair."

"Me?" He frowned. "You're the one who cancelled lunch on me."

She jerked her head up. "Because you left."

"I left because..." He shook his head and dropped his arms as he began to pace the small hallway. "I freaked." He shrugged before he turned to her. "You're the one who didn't want this to go any further. I tried to keep things light between us. I've done everything you asked. No one in my family knows about us. I fought the urge to buy you flowers and have them delivered. I've never wanted to buy flowers for a woman and had to hold back before." He shook his head and went back to pacing.

She stopped him by placing a hand on his shoulder. "George, what are you saying?"

He turned to her suddenly, dislodging her hand from his shoulder.

"Robin, I know you wanted to keep things between us..."—he shook his head— "quiet and... shallow, but I don't think I can..." He stopped when she started laughing almost hysterically.

There she was, standing in the darkened hallway, wrapped in nothing but a large white towel, her long gorgeous hair tied up in what could only be described as a rat's nest of a bun, without a stitch of makeup on, and he still believed her to be the most beautiful woman he'd ever seen.

Yeah, he was in trouble. Big trouble.

"What's so funny?" he asked when she took a gulp of air.

"You." She motioned to him and held her stomach before wiping a tear from her eyes. "You think that I..." She took a deep breath and then all the laughter fell away from her face. "I thought that's what you wanted. Everyone in town knows..." She bit her bottom lip and shook her head quickly from side to side.

"No." He took a step closer. "Go on. Everyone in town knows what?"

She closed her eyes as if trying to compose herself.

"Let me get dressed. Why don't you go on into the kitchen, grab a beer? I'll be right out. I can't—won't—do this standing in the hallway in a towel."

"I rather enjoy what you're wearing." He tried for humor and earned a slight smile. "But I'll grab a beer." He turned, but then stopped. "For what it's worth, I'm sorry I left yesterday."

Instead of answering, she nodded, walked into her room, and shut the door on him.

He headed into the kitchen, pulled open the fridge, and saw a case of his favorite beer. Seeing it, he realized that in the short time they'd been together, she knew even this about him.

Since he understood her, he poured a glass of her favorite wine and took a few moments to put some cheese and meat slices on a plate, along with some grapes.

He set everything down on the coffee table, then returned and grabbed the bag of her favorite cookies. Then he waited.

When she stepped out again, she wore dark gray

leggings and a large white T-shirt. She'd taken the time to braid her long hair, and it lay over her shoulder.

"What's all this?" she asked.

"If I know you, you won't have eaten anything since lunch." He motioned as he handed her the glass of wine.

She smiled. "Actually, I had a wonderful dinner."

He arched his eyebrows at her. "You did?"

"Yes, Kara sent me home with a plate, and I ate every bite."

His eyes narrowed. "Which you ate because you skipped breakfast and lunch?"

She closed her eyes. "Point taken." She sat down and sipped the wine, then grabbed a slice of cheese.

"I messed up," he admitted and watched a look of surprise cross her face.

"With?" she asked, reaching for a grape.

"I should have told you that my intentions about our arrangement had changed," he answered. She leaned back, holding her wine glass to her chest as her eyes roamed over his face.

"To?" she finally asked.

He set down his beer, reached up, took her glass from her, and pulled her up until they were so close, he could smell the jasmine on her skin.

"Whatever our journey was when we began, it's changed course. I think you feel it as much as I do. Trust me when I say that I'm not normally the kind of guy who sticks beyond a few weeks. The longest relationship of mine to date... is with you. I've never explored anything beyond casual before. In all honesty, I'm probably not going to be any good at it." His smile matched hers. "But if you're game, I'm willing to give it a try. I'm tired of hiding this"—he squeezed her hands gently— "from everyone. Who cares what the town thinks? What my family or yours think of our private lives."

"I've seen what happens when a new Jordan relationship comes to light in Pride." She shrugged slightly. "If you want to go through that"—her smile increased— "I'm game."

He pulled her into his arms and hugged her. "It was killing me, you know."

"What?" she asked as he buried his face into her braided hair.

"Not being with you. Thinking that you didn't want to be seen with me."

She chuckled. "What woman wouldn't want to be seen on the arm of a Jordan man?"

He pulled back and ran his eyes over her face before kissing her.

Even though it had only been twenty-four hours since the last time he'd done so, it was as if it had been a lifetime. He'd been starved for her.

"Let me stay tonight," he said between kisses.

"Yes," she sighed, "stay."

He questioned if she knew what she was agreeing to. He wanted to finish telling her how he felt. Hear her own feelings as well. But then she swung her leg up and over and climbed into his lap, and his mind went completely blank.

His hands moved to her hips, circling her narrow waist as she took the kiss deeper. Hoisting her up, he laid her gently on the sofa, covered her as his hands nudged those skintight leggings down until he cupped her, slid a finger into her.

She arched into him, moaned his name while her nails scraped against his skin. She pulled his shirt over his head.

He fumbled to unzip his jeans, to quickly slide on a condom, then cover her, fill her, be consumed and surrounded by her.

"This matters," he said next to her ear.

"Yes," she agreed as they both fell together.

His entire body and mind floated as he thought about just how wonderful it felt to be with Robin again. How close he'd come to losing this. Losing her. And it would have totally been his fault. There were a lot of things he could have done differently, and he was determined to start now.

"We should move," she said against his shoulder.

"Mm," he said before rolling over and lifting her into his arms. She laughed and then held onto him as he carried her into the bedroom and gently laid her on the bed.

He spent the entire night making love to the woman he cared about. It was one of the best nights of his life.

In the morning, he woke when his phone beeped with a meeting reminder.

"I have an hour till I'm supposed to be in the office," he said, leaning over and placing a kiss on Robin's lips. "Not a lot of time for both breakfast and..." He kissed her deeper. "So I'll have to grab some food on the run." He smiled down at her as her arms wrapped around his head and pulled him back to her.

An hour later, he jogged to his office in the same clothes he'd worn the night before, since he'd walked to her place. Even the light rain couldn't put a damper on his mood. When he passed All in Bloom, he quickly made a decision and stepped into his cousin's shop.

"Morning," Suzie said, glancing over from a rather large display of pastel-colored tulips.

"Morning." He smiled. Instantly, he realized he had no idea what Robin's favorite flowers were. Or even what her favorite color was.

"Need some help?" Suzie asked, walking over to him.

"Um." He was suddenly feeling a little overwhelmed. He had always known what his mother, his aunts, and even his cousins liked and had never had to guess about what to get them.

He thought about all the flowers he'd seen Robin around. Most of them had been for events.

He turned to Suzie and shrugged.

"What would you suggest I get?" he asked.

"For whom?" Suzie's eyes narrowed. "Your mother?"

"No." He cleared his throat. He remembered what he'd said to Robin last night. Knew his meaning. Even thought she had technically agreed to make their relationship public, he didn't want to reveal things just yet. Facts were facts. If he told Suzie now that he was buying flowers for Robin, then it would be clear to his cousin that they were seeing one another. It was also very clear to him that Suzie would turn around and tell the rest of his family.

"You should see your face," Suzie said with a chuckle. "You look as if you're trying to figure out a puzzle." She pointed at his face. "And like you're about to puke."

He rolled his eyes and took a deep breath. "I need to get flowers for someone special, but..." He tilted his head. "Do you have some sort of florist-client privilege code?"

Suzie laughed and leaned closer. "Want me to keep a secret?"

"Yes, please."

Suzie's eyes narrowed at him. "What do I get in return?" she asked.

"That knowledge ahead of the rest of the family," he responded, knowing it wouldn't be good enough.

When Suzie shook her head, he sighed and crossed his arms over her chest.

"My office could use some fresh flowers," he admitted.

"Weekly?"

"Biweekly," he countered. When she opened her mouth to turn him down, he sighed. "Along with a few plants. You know, the green kind that need watering all the time."

A smile flashed quickly on her lips. "Okay, who are we shopping for today?"

He glanced around the empty shop and leaned closer.

"Robin. I have no idea what her favorite—"

"Finally! I knew it!" Suzie laughed and turned to walk over to the wall of tulips. "These should do it." She started gathering up a bundle of yellow flowers. "Robin is a stickler for what's in season," she said. "Even though it's still early for these, I have connections and just got them," she told him as she worked. "Want these delivered?" she asked over her shoulder.

He started to say no, but Suzie's eyes narrowed again. "Yes, sure."

"Good." She smiled and turned back to the task. "Now, you can write your message on one of the cards up there, seal it in an envelope." She motioned to the front counter where a stand held all sorts of small cards and little envelopes. "I'll have Kate deliver these when she gets in."

"Are you sure you don't want to read what I write?" he teased, earning him a crossed-eyed tongue-sticking-out face from his cousin.

He walked over and pulled out the first little card from the display. Seeing the red hearts on it, he quickly put it back and grabbed one with a floral design instead.

What should he write? Thanks for the hot sex last night and agreeing to let me tell everyone I get to bang you?

God, he was in trouble. And very bad at writing love notes.

CHAPTER FIFTEEN

Robin's morning was going a lot better than yesterday morning. She practically glided into her little office in the back of the barn, then stopped dead in her tracks when she noticed the massive bundle of tulips sitting in a vase on her desk.

"Kara?" she called out, knowing her sister had gotten there almost half an hour before her.

"Yes?" her sister replied back.

"What are these...?" She moved towards them and noticed the envelope with her name on it.

She'd assumed that the flowers had gotten misplaced or left behind after last night's event. Taking the note, she smiled down at her name.

"Those came for you. Kate dropped them off a few minutes ago." Her sister stopped beside her. "I'm itching to know who they are from, but Kate warned me that I'd get the wrath of Suzie if I opened the note."

Robin leaned down and smelled the sweet scent of the yellow happy faces of the flowers and smiled.

"So, are you going to tell me who they are from?" Kara asked.

Glancing sideways at her sister she smiled. "Maybe." She held the card to her chest. "Go away now. I'll decide later." She waved her sister away.

Kara narrowed her eyes and sighed as she left the room. "Fine, be that way," her sister said, sulking.

Robin smiled even more when she opened the card and read George's note.

"I know that I'm a few days late, but I'm happy that I can finally say Happy Valentine's to you properly. -G"

"G?" Kara said directly from over her shoulder.

Robin jumped and hugged the note to her chest again.

"None of your business." She rolled her eyes at her sister. "Go away."

"Not until you tell me who G is." Kara crossed her good arm over her bad one. "Are you seeing someone?" Her sister's eyes narrowed. "Why didn't you tell me?"

"Because, as I said, it's none of your business." She replied with a smile as she sat down at her desk. She moved the vase of flowers around until she was pleased that she would get to enjoy seeing them all day long.

"I told you about me and Conner," Kara replied. "The moment..." She dropped off. "I told you about us."

"Yeah, and that was your prerogative. Just as it's mine to keep this secret until we decide to tell everyone." She glanced up at her sister. "Together."

"Fine." Kara shrugged and turned around. "I already know, anyway. Everyone in town has for a while."

"Oh?" Robin asked. She could tell her sister was lying.

Kara turned to her and then gasped. "George?" Robin's heart skipped. "He's the only man whose name starts with a G that I know." Her sister moved back to the edge of her desk. "George Stevens? Robin, he's..." She could see the concern flood her sister's eyes. "Sweetie, he's not the type I expected you'd go for."

"I know." Robin leaned back and looked at the flowers with a slight smile. "But there it is. At first, he was just a... distraction." She shrugged and turned back to her sister. "Then, things changed. He changed." She leaned her elbows on the desk. "We broke things off, then..." She motioned to the flowers. "You called him last night and told him I was sick." She narrowed her eyes at Kara. "Why did you call him?"

"Because I knew the two of you were friends. I had no idea that you were... together." Kara shrugged. "I mean, you went sailing with him..." Her eyes narrowed. "How long has this togetherness been going on?"

This time, Robin shrugged. "A few months."

"Months!" Kara sat on the edge of her desk and ran her fingers over the yellow petals of the tulips. "Months," she said softly. "Is it serious?"

"No, it's nothing really." Robin instantly denied it as she played over George's words last night. Was it serious? Sure, he'd agreed to make their relationship public and to continue seeing one another. That didn't mean it was serious. Certainly not as serious as Kara and Conner's relationship.

George hadn't professed his love for her. Even in the note he'd written, he hadn't signed it, love George. Just -G.

Did she love George? She didn't think so. Not yet at least. Sure, she had a great fondness for him, enough that she didn't want their relationship to end as it had the night before.

She'd been walking on air earlier that morning just knowing that they were back together and that she was going to be able to continue seeing him, enjoying him in her bed. Now, however, thanks to her sister, she was worried that she'd once again moved the relationship goal up too far.

She shook off the mood and was keeping busy by balancing the books and moving events around on the calendar when a bride called her, crying and claiming that her soon-to-be husband had cheated on her and that the wedding was off. Soon after, the mother of the bride called and claimed that her daughter was just being emotional and that the wedding wasn't off.

Soon after that, she received a call from the groom explaining that his bride was just getting cold feet.

She didn't know what to think and grayed out the event, keeping the date in her calendar just in case.

When a knock sounded at her door, she glanced up to see George standing there, smiling at her.

"Have time to break for lunch?" he asked her.

"Lunch?" She glanced at the clock hanging next to the doorway and realized she'd been on the phone practically all morning long. "Sure." She stood up, stretched, and groaned at her sore muscles from sitting so long.

He walked over and wrapped his arms around her.

"Did you like the flowers?" he asked.

"Love them." She smiled back at him. "Thank you."

He glanced back. "My cousin Suzie has been sworn to secrecy."

She groaned slightly. "My sister knows. She read your note over my shoulder."

"It's okay," he smiled. "We did agree to make it known. I had just hoped to tell my family all at once. For now, how about we show everyone by heading down to Baked and sitting in a back booth and necking while we wait for our pizza?"

She smiled and leaned up to kiss him. "That's one way to tell everyone we're..." She raised her eyebrows.

"Seeing one another?" he suggested.

"That will do it."

She'd never really felt nervous on a lunch date before. But sitting in the back booth of Baked, snuggling up to George, she felt more nervous than she had on her very first date when she'd been fifteen.

"People are staring," she said, looking up into his eyes.

George's arm was wrapped around her tight. Even though he hadn't kissed her yet, their body language was obvious to anyone who passed by.

"Let them." He looked down into her eyes. "Does it bother you?"

"No." She shook her head slightly. "But if you'd kiss me, I might forget anyone else is around."

He smiled and leaned down to brush his lips across hers. "Just kissing you makes me feel like the entire world is just us." He leaned further into her and kissed her until they both heard someone clear their throat.

"Go away," George said without looking to see who it was.

Robin chuckled slightly, then gasped when she saw his mother, Lacey Stevens, standing at the edge of their booth, looking down at them.

Crap. Well, they had agreed to let their relationship out to his family. And seeing as Lacey was the head of his family, she supposed it was a good place to start.

Robin tried to pull away from George, only to have his arms tighten around her.

"Mother." George motioned to the other side of the booth. "Care to join us for lunch?"

"I'd say yes, but I'm picking up a few pies for the office. We have a little..." Lacey's eyes narrowed slightly. "Kafuffle to deal with. So, you two are finally making it official?"

"Finally?" George asked. Robin had a sinking feeling in her gut.

"Well, of course I've known all along. I'm your mother and I have eyes." She narrowed them further at her son, before turning to her as her smile grew. "I'm so happy you've decided to give my son a chance. I promise you he's not a complete idiot. Your sister"—she motioned to Robin—"tells me he finally had some flowers delivered today." Her eyes moved back to her son. "Two days late."

"Mother," George said with a tone that was almost a warning.

Lacey waved her hand as if brushing him off. "Maybe

now he'll invite you to a family dinner? Say, this Friday night?"

Robin winced. "I've got the McGowen's wedding."

"Oh, right. How about brunch on Sunday?" Lacey suggested quickly.

"I'll be there," Robin said after George nodded to her slightly.

"Good, now enjoy your lunch." Lacey turned around and headed back up to get several boxes of pizza before leaving.

"That was fun," George said, getting her to laugh.

"I like your mom. I always have, but that was..." She took a deep breath.

"I'm sorry," he said softly.

"Don't be." She smiled. "Wait until my parents..." She groaned when her eyes moved past him and fell on her parents talking to Lacey outside the pizzeria. "You won't have to wait long." She nodded. George followed her gaze outside. "For what's about to happen, I'm totally sorry," she said as her parents' gazes moved past Lacey and locked with hers.

"Hey, that was just my mom," he reminded her, taking her hand under the table as her parents stepped inside. "Wait until the rest of my family hears."

"So." Robin's mother stopped at the table, a little breathless. "It's true?"

"Mom, Dad, why don't you sit down." She motioned to the booth. "Our pizza should be ready soon."

"Your father will order our food." Her mother glanced over to her father, who quickly nodded and disappeared. "So, is it true?" she asked again.

"What?" Robin asked, squeezing George's hand under the table.

"Mrs. Jenkins, I wanted to..." George started.

"Shush." Her mother waved him off with a smile. "I want to hear it from my own daughter's mouth."

Robin was momentarily mortified, until George chuckled and leaned back in the booth.

"George and I are seeing one another," she blurted out.

Her mother shocked her again by waving her hand. "Not that, I think the entire town has known that for weeks." Her mother scooted into the booth and leaned closer. "I'm talking about the Maddison's wedding being called off. Did Troy Maddison really cheat on Jenna? Have they really called the wedding off? You know that the Maddisons are old friends of ours. I can't believe little Troy would do such a thing."

Robin relaxed and for the next half an hour she filled her mother in on all the phone calls she'd handled that morning. It was sort of strange that her parents didn't really mention or call out her and George's relationship, other than to say that everyone had already known about it.

Almost all the conversation during lunch was filled with gossip. Gossip that had nothing to do with her relationship with George.

"That was fun," George said as they walked back. "And here I was thinking I was going to get the third degree. If not by your mother, then at least by your father. I thought he would demand to know my intentions at least."

She laughed. "My parents have never really been so hands on that they would embarrass us, but still, I had expected that they'd at least talk about us."

"I'm glad they didn't." He sighed. "Just knowing that, come Sunday, you'll have to deal with the rest of my family..." He sighed. "If I know my mother, it won't be just my sister and Corey there this weekend."

"I've been around your entire family before, remember?" she said, as they walked into the barn.

"Yeah." He stopped her by pulling her into his arms and kissing her. "I've got to get back to the office, but I was hoping... Will I see you tonight?"

She smiled. "I should be done around ten."

"I'll come by your place." He kissed her again.

"Oh god, give a girl a warning next time," Kara said with a groan.

George chuckled as he stepped away from her. "Later," he said to her, then smiled at Kara.

They watched as George disappeared, then her sister turned to her and playfully slapped her on the shoulder.

"That did not look like it was nothing." She narrowed her eyes at her. "Talk about hot and steamy." Her sister fanned her face for show, causing Robin to chuckle.

"Go away, I have work." She nudged her sister out of her office.

"Okay, but there's a man here for you." Kara shrugged. "Says he would only talk to you." She leaned in. "Maybe you shouldn't have sent George off yet?"

"It's probably just the Maddisons. Mom mentioned they were sending someone to talk about possibly moving the wedding back." She held up her hand before her sister could ask what was going on with the longtime family friends. "Don't ask."

CHAPTER SIXTEEN

George smiled the entire way back to his office. He knew that he probably looked like a goon but he didn't care. Robin made him feel like there was something better in life and just knowing that she was going to allow him to be around to enjoy that feeling longer made him happy.

The moment he walked into his office, Mia got his attention. Looks could be deceiving with the woman. She was tall and frail looking, but moved around the office full of purpose and experience.

"You have a call. She claims it's an emergency." She held up the phone to him.

Worry had him rushing forward and taking the phone.

"This is George."

"George, you'd better come back." It was Kara. The two sisters sounded so much alike until you grew close to either of them. Then the subtle difference in their looks and their voices was obvious.

"What's wrong?" he asked.

"I'm not a hundred percent sure. Robin had a visit from... well, I don't know who. But after, she locked herself in her office. She slammed the door on the man. Now she won't open up to talk to me. I'm afraid it was one of Carson's men."

"I'll be right there." He handed the phone back to Mia. "Move my meeting back," he said as he rushed out the front door again.

He ran as fast as he could, reaching the barn doors in half the time it had taken him to walk back to the office. Kara was standing there, waiting for him.

"Did you see him? You must have passed him on your way here. Dark gray sedan?" She motioned to the empty parking lot.

"No." He'd been so worried about Robin, he hadn't even looked out for anyone on the road. When he knocked on Robin's door, she called out.

"Go away, Kara. I need time to think."

"It's me," he said, and waited until she unlocked the office door.

He could see the worry and fear in her eyes and knew that her sister had been correct. Whoever she'd met with, Robin was scared.

He gathered her in his arms. "What's wrong?"

Robin's eyes moved past him to her sister.

"I'm not going to let you shut me out," Kara said, stepping into the room and crossing her arms.

He felt Robin sigh and relent. "Come on in." She stepped away from his hold.

They both waited as she moved to sit behind her desk, then she pushed a folder towards him. "I was just composing myself enough to call you," she admitted, her eyes locked on his. "I just had a visit from a lawyer." She held up her hand. "No, I don't think it was Thomas Carson, or the one you met with your uncle. This man seemed to know just how to intimidate me." She handed him a card.

He read the name and frowned down at it.

"Why was Joe Nelson visiting you? He's a county code enforcement lawyer."

She sat, took a couple deep breaths, and then blurted out. "He's shutting us down."

"What?" Kara practically screamed it. "He can't do that."

George opened the folder and quickly scanned through the paperwork.

He glanced up at Robin. "You have your business and liquor license?"

"Yes." She motioned to the papers hanging on the wall. He moved over and scanned the document she had hanging on the wall behind her.

"They're up to date." He scanned the documents again. "Did you show Nelson these?"

"Yes. He claimed that there was no record of them at city hall and that until this mess is figured out, we have to cancel all of our events." Robin's voice hitched, so he walked around and pulled her into his arms and held onto her.

"I know Nelson personally. I'm going to head down to city hall and straighten this all out," he told Robin, then glanced over to Kara. "What time is your next event?"

She glanced at her watch. "Two hours." She bit her bottom lip.

"How could this happen?" Robin asked against his chest.

"I'm not sure, but I'm going to have to borrow those." He motioned to the licenses.

Robin nodded and stepped away again. "I—"

"Don't thank me just yet. I'll let you know the moment I find out anything." He walked over, took the licenses, put them in the folder, and tucked it under his arm. As he walked out, he called Mia.

"Cancel all my meetings. Something has come up," he told her.

"Um, well, there's a gentleman by the name of Joe Nelson here to—"

"Keep him there. I'll be there in five." He started running back to his office again.

When he hit the end of the street, he slowed his pace down and allowed his breathing to calm so that by the time he walked into his office again, he was back under control.

"Nelson." He shook the older man's hand and motioned for the man to follow him back to his office.

Joe Nelson had gone to high school with George's mother. He was a second-generation Pride resident who had, much like George, disappeared into the city for a few years for college and to pass the bar exam before returning back to Pride and settling into a position down at city hall. Over the years, the man's job qualifications had seemed to shrink. So had his knowledge about new laws.

"What can I help you with today, Nelson?" George asked, after setting Robin's file down on his desk. He could tell that Joe noticed it, but he didn't say anything.

"Well, I'm here about your business license, George. There seems to be some mix-up down at the county," Nelson started.

"Oh?" George could guess what was coming next. He knew for a fact that everything was up to date, since he'd just gotten all his paperwork only a few weeks ago. "Problems?" he asked.

"Yes, I'm afraid I'll have to shut you down. At least until we get things squared away," Nelson said.

Just then, his office door barged open and Suzie rushed in. "I don't care if he's in a meeting..." she was saying to Mia. When his cousin's eyes fell on Joe, sitting in the chair across from George, her eyes narrowed. Then she turned to him.

"That man just told me I have to shut my business down," Suzie said, pointing at Nelson.

George turned back to the man. "Okay, Joe, want to tell me what this is really about? So far this afternoon you have hit three businesses, that I know of, all with up-to-date business licenses."

He waited and, for the first time, the man appeared uneasy.

"I'm just doing my job," Nelson replied.

Suzie seemed flustered, but thankfully remained quiet.

"Okay," George said after a moment. "I'm just going to make a quick call." He picked up his office phone and punched his mother's cell number in.

"Hello?" His mother sounded flustered and busy.

"I know you are probably busy, but I've got Joe Nelson in my office..."

"Son of a..." His mother broke in. "Don't let that man go. Aiden and I will be right there," his mother said before hanging up.

George motioned to the free chair. "Suzie, why don't you take a chair." He turned to Mia, who was still standing in the hallway. "Would you call Robin and her sister and ask that they join us here as well?"

Mia nodded and rushed back down the hallway.

"I don't have time." Nelson started to stand up, but when George cocked an eyebrow at him, the man sat back down.

"The mayor and the sheriff will be here in just a few moments," he said to the room.

Robin and her sister walked in almost a full minute before his mother and Aiden did. Thankfully, he'd moved everyone into the conference room before the real show had started.

"What on god's green earth are you doing, Joe?" his mother asked as she stormed into the room.

"My job," Joe had responded. "Something you seem to not want to do."

"I told you, it's just a computer glitch. You can't go around shutting down people's businesses." His mother motioned to the crowd of people now streaming into his offices. You've pissed off a lot of locals. People who you depend on daily. I made it clear that we'd get this straightened out."

"It's not a glitch. There are no records. Period.

Someone dropped the ball in this town, and it won't be me taking the fall. I know the law." He practically yelled the last statement.

"Why don't you fill us all in on what's going on?" George asked his mother.

Even though Lacey Jordan stood only five feet, four inches tall, she held the attention of everyone in the room. When she spoke, people listened. It was one of the reasons she'd become one of Pride's most beloved mayors.

"Sometime prior to lunchtime, there appears to have been a computer glitch that wiped out all of the town's business licenses for the past year." She held up her hand before anyone was given a chance to speak. "Currently, Josh Williams from Internet Security Systems is working on resolving the issue."

"It's not a computer glitch." Nelson stood up suddenly. "This is coming down from the county. These licenses are void." He motioned to the stack of copies George had given him of his, Suzie's, and Robin's licenses.

At this point, several people in the room started shouting over one another.

His mother held up her hands, and when that didn't do the trick, she whistled an ear-piercing whistle. Everyone grew quiet again.

"Whatever this is, it is just a glitch. Rest assured that this matter is an internal issue. All of your business licenses are still valid. Even if I have to type them out myself. Go back to your businesses. Open your doors. Sell. Bake," she said, glancing between his sister Lilly and then over at Sara. "Do business as usual." She turned on

Nelson. "You and I need to have a talk," she said, pointing at the man's chest. "Now." Without waiting for a response, she marched from the room and headed into his office.

Since it was his office, he stood and followed her, making sure Nelson did as well.

"I'll let you know," he mouthed to Robin as he shut his office door.

Over the course of his entire twenty-five years, he had never seen his mother as pissed as she was now. There had been plenty that his mother had yelled at him for over the years, but nothing that had caused a little twitch in her left eye.

"How dare you," his mother said once it was just the four of them in the room. Aiden had followed his mother. His mother turned on Nelson. "I told you I had this under control. You went behind my back and caused a mob of angry business owners."

"I was doing—"

"Don't pull that crap on me," his mother countered. "Your job is what I say it is." She took a deep breath. "Now, we can do one of two things. You can return to your office, pack your things, and take an early retirement or..." Nelson started to open his mouth to object, but his mother narrowed her eyes. "Or," she said a little louder, "I can fire you on the spot for insubordination. It's up to you."

"You can't—" Nelson started to move forward, but both Aiden and George moved to block the man. Instantly, his mother pushed them both aside.

"When I need protecting, I'll call your father," she

said to him. "As mayor of this town, I have the authority to hire and fire anyone who works under my office. What's your decision?"

"I'll pack up and write my resignation," Nelson said after a moment.

"Good choice." Lacey nodded to Aiden. "Aiden here will make sure you get everything you need from your office."

Once Aiden and Nelson left the office, his mother collapsed into one of his chairs.

Smiling, he walked over, sat down at his desk, pulled out his emergency supplies from his bottom drawer, and handed his mother a chocolate bar.

His mother leaned across the way, snatched the bar from his hands, and sank back to enjoy the treat.

"Rough day in the office?" he asked, biting into his own chocolate bar.

His mother glared at him, took a bite, then smiled. "I knew I hadn't raised a fool," she said with a sigh. "That man..."—she motioned to the door with her chocolate—"has caused a world of worry today."

"What happened with the computers? Do you think you were hacked?" he asked.

"What I think is irrelevant. It's what Josh finds that matters. Trust me, I don't doubt that by the end of today, he'll know exactly what happened and who is responsible."

"It's why I trusted him to install all my new systems here." He motioned to his new state-of-the-art computer. "The man knows his business."

"One thing I'd say about Nelson, he works fast. By

the time I had four business owners down in my office, he'd already hit half of the town. Finishing up with the three of you down here." She sighed.

"I wasn't worried," he admitted then remembered how worried Robin had been. How much she and her sister relied on keeping their doors open. "I have friends in high places."

CHAPTER SEVENTEEN

Now that her business and liquor licenses were hanging back on her wall, Robin felt a little more settled. Still, for the following few nights, nightmares of losing her business filled her dreams.

The news of Joe Nelson's fiasco traveled all over town, as did news of his forced early retirement.

She'd heard from George that the city's and county's computer systems had been hacked and that Josh Williams was working hard at tracking down the perpetrator and, more importantly, the reason.

"Apparently, it's a mess," George told her a few days later while they sat in the bakery enjoying some hot cinnamon rolls and coffee. She'd spent the night at his place and, had to admit, she was starting to feel more at home there than she had at first. For one thing, he had a better sofa and TV than she did. "Everyone in town will have to scan their licenses and email them in, just so they have records of them. It's that or reapply after the system is fully locked down. I guess one good thing came out of this. Josh now has the contract to secure the city and county systems." He chuckled.

"I can't believe how scared I was of losing my business," she admitted. "I was about to call you, knowing you would help, but I never really thought..." She shook her head.

He reached across the table and took her hand in his. "I've gone over all your paperwork. You have nothing to fear," he assured her.

"I know. But it doesn't stop my brain from going over all the possibilities."

George smiled at her. "That's why I'm here." He lifted her hand to his lips.

"Well, isn't this cozy." A man walked up to their table and stopped to stare down at George.

She felt his hand tense inside hers, then relax slightly before dropping away.

"Can I help you?" George said, sounding a little unsure.

"I would hope so. You're that fancy new lawyer that came in from the city?" the man said with a grin. Robin noticed a few missing teeth in the middle-aged man's mouth.

"I am. George..." Before he could say anything else, the man moved forward quickly. Robin's scream hadn't even left her before George's blood splattered all over her face. There was a loud smacking sound when the man's fist plowed into George's nose.

In the next seconds, there was a blur of activity as George pushed out of the booth and tackled the man to the ground. Two other bodies seemed to materialize out of nowhere to help George.

"That's for Laura," the man was screaming. "You took my wife," he said over and over as George, Aiden, and Corey held the man down.

"Are you okay?" Suzie asked Robin. It was then that Robin noticed that both Suzie and Lilly had been sitting at a table across the way with their husbands. She'd been so consumed by George's attention earlier that she hadn't noticed who else was in the bakery.

"He just…" She felt her throat close up. "George?" She pushed out of the booth when she noticed blood spurting out of George's nose. "Here." She took some fresh napkins from their table and covered his nose. "You're bleeding."

"Do you have him?" George asked Aiden and Corey before taking the napkins from her and holding them over his nose. "Son of a…" He broke off when he noticed a few families in the dining area. "I think he broke my nose."

The man continued to scream about a woman named Laura and how George had stolen her from him.

"Why don't you head over and have your dad take a look at that. We've got Larry here." Aiden motioned to the man. "Witnessed the entire thing." Aiden turned to the man. "Hey, hotshot, next time you want to assault someone, make sure the sheriff isn't sitting five feet away." Aiden shook his head.

"Thanks," George said while pinching his nose.

Robin grabbed up his coat and followed him outside.

She had to jog a little to keep up with his long strides

as he made his way down the street towards his father's medical clinic.

"What was that about?" she asked him.

"Damned if I know," he said, walking and trying to keep his nose up in the air.

"Your coat." She worried that the freezing air was affecting him.

"I'm okay. I think the adrenaline is keeping me warm," he said through the blood-soaked tissues.

They were less than half a block away from the clinic when they noticed his father standing out on the sidewalk, waiting for them.

"He got you good," his father said as George removed the soaked tissue. "Becca from the bakery called me and filled me in on what happened."

"Yeah, sucker punched me while I was sitting down," George said with a sigh.

"Larry Butcher has always been a coward," Aaron said with a groan. "It's not as bad as it looks." he said smoothly. "Come on in, I'll set it back to right and check you out." His father turned and they followed him into the clinic.

She'd been inside the small medical facility a few times. When she'd been a kid one vacation, she'd gotten the flu and had run a fever, prompting her parents to take her to see Doctor Stevens. The last time she'd been inside was shortly after they had finished work on the barn. She'd somehow walked into a nail sticking out of a wall and had cut her leg. Thankfully, the doctor had used super glue after cleaning the cut instead of stitches.

"Can I come back?" she asked George's father.

He looked to George, who nodded, so she followed the two men through the little lobby, down the hallway, and into one of the smaller examination rooms.

George jumped up on the table like he'd been there a million times. Then it hit her. This had no doubt been his second home growing up. How many times had he been here? Hurt or not.

She sat in the chair as his father examined him, then set George's broken nose. She was very impressed when George only flinched as his father set the broken cartilage. The bleeding stopped instantly.

"Better?" his dad asked him.

"Much." George sighed and relaxed back. "Thanks." He started to get up, but his father stopped him.

"You know the drill. You've been assaulted. Aiden would skin me alive if I didn't do a full exam and check you out for a concussion."

George groaned, but relaxed back. Robin hadn't been worried about anything other than the broken nose, but now she worried that there was more wrong with him. She remembered hearing the loud cracking sound when he'd been hit.

"Everything looks good," Aaron was saying when the door burst open and Lacey stormed in.

"Why is it I have to hear about our son being assaulted from the sheriff?" she asked the room. Her eyes scanned over Robin quickly before she moved over to wrap her arms around her son.

"I'll get blood..." he started to say, trying to hold her back, but his mother just shushed him and held onto him.

"He had a broken nose. I'll want to see you in a week.

You know the drill—be careful with it, ice, Tylenol, and"
—Aaron smiled and winked at Robin— "be careful when you kiss him."

She smiled a little and nodded.

"Other than that, he's healthy." Aaron walked over and took Lacey by the shoulders and held onto her. "Our boy's okay."

"Yes." She nodded and allowed her husband to lead her from the room.

When the door shut behind his parents, she stood up, walked over to George, and wrapped her arms around him.

"Are you okay?" she asked as she held onto him.

"Yeah," he sighed. "He caught me off guard."

She leaned back, locked eyes with him, and asked. "Want to tell me who Laura is?" she asked, earning a chuckle from him.

"It didn't dawn on me until my dad said Larry's last name. Laura Butcher, Larry's wife, came into my office this morning and started the process of filing for divorce from her husband," he said with a sigh.

"Come on, Rocky," she said as she reached up and wiggled his jaw. "How about we play hooky today?"

"Can't..." he started to say, but then he sighed. "Okay, since I know there is no way I can get past my parents without agreeing to taking the day off, I'll call Mia and have her move all my appointments to tomorrow." He pulled out his cell phone, and she listened to him talk to his assistant. Then she pulled out her phone and sent a text message to her sister.

Even though she had an event later that night, she

figured Kara and Emma could handle most of the setup. Her sister responded that the news of what had happened had already reached her and that they could handle everything themselves. When she asked how George was doing, she responded with a picture of him smiling and giving a thumbs up.

"Okay, so if we're going to play hooky..." He jumped off the table and wrapped his arms around her. "Let's do this properly."

"Oh?" she asked, a little worried when he swayed slightly. She wrapped her arms around him as he started walking towards the door.

"How about we head over to Patty's, grab some ice cream and some cookies, and spend the day in bed, watching movies?" he finished a little louder than he'd started, since both of his parents were watching and listening.

"That sounds good," she agreed.

"Don't forget the ice and Tylenol," his father added.

"Right," he agreed.

"I'll have Aiden call you if he needs anything from you," his father said as they walked outside.

"Something tells me they are still going to worry," she said, holding on to him.

He chuckled. "If I know my parents, they'll probably drop by my place later to make sure I'm resting. So, why fight it?" He shrugged. "Besides, spending an entire day in bed with you"—he wiggled his eyebrows then winced — "is my idea of a great day."

The moment they stepped into Patty's store, they were bombarded with well-wishers and questions.

"Why don't you go grab what we need. I'll answer questions." He squeezed her hand.

As she walked around and tossed a bunch of junk food into her cart, she noticed the crowd growing as everyone listened to George tell his story.

"You're with him?" a thin blonde woman asked her in a hushed tone.

Robin couldn't remember having ever seen the woman in town before but nodded.

"Yes, George and I are seeing one another," she answered.

"I'm Laura," she said softly. "I... wanted to apologize to George, but..." She glanced over at the crowd.

"You have nothing to apologize about," Robin assured the woman.

"My husband... Larry." She shook her head slightly. "He has a temper. It's why I'm divorcing him."

Robin ran her eyes over the woman and realized that Laura was probably younger than she appeared. She'd gauged Larry to be in his late forties, but if you took away the worried look, added a good haircut, clothes, and some makeup, Laura was probably in her mid-thirties. The woman could, with those changes, be described as pretty.

Robin reached out and touched the woman's arm. "I'm sure that George feels the same way as I do. You have nothing to apologize for. This isn't your doing." She decided to change gears. "Tell me you have a safe place to stay?"

The woman shrugged slightly. "I'm staying with my cousin. For now. Until I can find work and save up enough to get my own place."

"What kind of work?" Robin asked.

"I... used to work at the Oar as a waitress. I was going to apply there, but now..." Her eyes moved back to George.

"Why don't you stop by my business, Sunset Weddings today. My sister and I have been looking for a few more staff members to help out during bigger events. The least you can do is fill out an application."

"Really?" Laura asked, her voice rising slightly. "I've heard all about your place. I could only wish to work some place so... romantic." She sighed.

Robin smiled. "I'll let my sister Kara know you'll stop by today." She pulled out her phone and sent a quick text message. "There, it's done. Stop by when you can. Now, I'd better go save George before this ice cream melts. It was nice meeting you."

"You, too." Laura smiled and nodded.

"What was that about?" George asked her when she pulled him through the checkout line, and they started towards his place with two bags of junk food.

As they walked to his place, she filled him in on what she and Laura had talked about.

"I don't blame her," he said, unlocking his door and letting her in.

"Of course, you don't."

She could tell he was hurting now. He moved like a man in pain. Two dark circles had started forming under his eyes and the bridge of his nose was slightly swollen.

"Here." She took the bag from him and set it on the kitchen counter next to the one she'd set down. Then she reached inside one of them, pulled out a bag of frozen peas, and handed it to him along with a fresh bottle of Tylenol. "Go into the living room, turn on the television, relax while I put this stuff away." She handed him a soda and then nudged him towards the sofa.

She had to admit, this place was a lot bigger than the cottage. The kitchen was twice the size of her own.

As she moved around, putting the items away, she realized she'd gotten spoiled staying there with him. Not only did George have a bigger and newer mattress, the shower in this place was just freaking amazing. Shower heads sprayed her from every direction and there was a large seat, which she and George had enjoyed on many occasions.

Once everything was put away, she stepped into the living room and smiled when she saw him relaxing back on the sofa, his feet up on the coffee table, a bag of peas covering his entire face as the news played on the television.

Before she said anything, she snapped a picture of him and sent it to his mother with a short text message.

"Rest assured, he's taken care of."

"How are you feeling?" she asked George.

He didn't move as he answered. "I feel like I was sucker punched and had my nose broken." Then he patted the spot next to him. "Come sit next to me. Find something for us to watch."

She sat down, placed a soft kiss on his forehead, then took the remote from him.

She toed off her shoes and covered them both with the blanket that lay over the back of his sofa.

"I bought something to make lunch and dinner. We

didn't get to finish our breakfast, so let me know when you're hungry," she said.

He nudged the bag of peas aside and looked at her.

"Why don't you move in here?" he surprised her by asking.

"What?" She shook her head and chuckled. "You mean, until you feel better?"

"No, I mean, move in. I mean, going between here and your place is exhausting. When we stay at the cottage, well, your work is only a few steps away. Not that I don't like the little place. The view is really cool. But this place is twice the size, we have a fenced yard if you want a dog, and once the place up in Hidden Cove is done, we can transition up there." He shrugged and watched her.

She'd listened to his reasoning and agreed with everything, but still, this was moving all too fast. Wasn't it? Knowing that he wanted her to live with him warmed her but scared her as well.

Part of her didn't want to let go of the cottage. It had been her first home. Her first purchase. She knew without a doubt that she wouldn't sell the place. Since it sat so close to the venue, she couldn't imagine anyone living there.

"You could rent the cottage out," he said, as if reading her mind. "Haven't you mentioned a few times that out-of-town guests have been looking for places to stay? I know each time you have a big wedding, my aunt's B and B is filled. Why not rent the cabin out as well? Make a little extra cash?"

She hadn't thought of that idea. Why hadn't she? It

would be perfect. With the prospect of the extra money, she could have the entire cottage outfitted with some new furniture. Maybe even hire Blake as interior designer to set the place up, redecorate it as a show piece.

Then her mind snapped into gear. George was asking her to move in with him. She turned and looked at him.

"That's a pretty big step. Are you sure you don't have a concussion?" she asked.

He smiled and wrapped his arm around her shoulder to pull her closer after he set the bag of peas down on the sofa next to him.

"I'm sure," he said softly, then he nudged her closer until he could kiss her softly on the lips.

She was careful not to get anywhere near his nose, which was now looking redder and a lot more swollen than it had before.

"Moving in with one another is a way bigger step than letting our families know we're seeing one another," she pointed out.

"It is," he agreed. "But I think it's a good step. Don't you?"

Her eyes ran over his face. Reaching up, she cupped his chin and nudged it from side to side. "Your dad did a good job putting it back into place. It looks straight."

"You're stalling," he said with a sigh. "That's not a good sign."

She smiled. "Yes." She nodded, causing his eyebrows to shoot up.

"Yes? As in, yes, that's not a good sign?" he asked, causing her to laugh.

"Yes, I'll move in with you," she corrected. "But it may take a while," she warned.

He pulled her close and kissed her again. This time he winced and pulled back in pain.

"Sorry," she apologized. "How bad is it?"

"Not as bad as it would have been if you'd said no." He sighed and pulled her back down to sit beside her.

CHAPTER EIGHTEEN

For the next two days, George's face stung like a bitch. It wasn't the first time his nose had been broken, so he'd instantly known it had snapped.

His father had set it back when he'd been eleven, just like he'd set it the other day. George had no doubt that he'd have a straight nose once all the swelling and bruising went down. His dad was that good of a doctor. And a father.

Saturday, the day after the event at Sara's Nook, his office was flooded with new client calls. Word was out. He now had more clients than he could handle. Most of the calls were simple requests to update wills or file legal paperwork, but others were more in depth, such as representing people in court cases.

He was thankful when Robin brought a large bag of her items over to his place the following night. He enjoyed seeing her shampoos and bottles in his bathroom and had helped her clear out half of his dresser for her. Since he'd only had a few suits and dress clothes hanging up in the closet, he easily shifted those items to the closet in the second bedroom to give her the entire walk-in closet in the main bedroom.

She'd tried to convince him that she didn't need the space, but he reminded her that he'd grown up with a sister and knew how much space women needed for their things.

Besides, she had all those fancy dresses she wore for work, and the big closet was a perfect space for it all.

He figured she'd take her time moving the rest of her things in and didn't want to push her. He offered to help her move some of the bigger items, but she'd assured him that most of the stuff wouldn't be making the journey.

Just as long as she was wrapped around him each night, he didn't care.

When Sunday brunch came around, he drove them out to his parents' place. He'd patiently watched her change outfits five times and held in a chuckle when she finally decided to wear the first outfit she'd tried on.

"We should have brought them flowers," she said as he pulled in and parked next to his father's truck. His aunts' and uncles' cars weren't there, but he that they would most likely have walked over and were now inside his parents' house.

"Trust me, with a florist in the family, I guarantee my mother's house is full of fresh bouquets," he said with a chuckle. "This wine is the best gift." He reached back and took the bottle. "It's my mother's favorite."

"I'll make a note of it," she responded with a smile.

"Have I mentioned that you look amazing?" He brushed a finger down her arm.

"Several times, but a woman never tires of hearing it." She smiled back at him.

He leaned in and brushed a kiss across her lips. He had to be careful not to brush his nose since it was still tender.

"Is there anything I need to know before we head in?" she surprised him by asking.

"Know? Let's see, my mother is a wonderful cook, my dad will probably ask you a million questions to ensure that I've been taken care of..." He motioned to his face. "Oh, and don't get Ruth started on belly rubs." He leaned over and opened his door. "She's the dog," he said with a chuckle.

He couldn't count the number of times he'd sat around his family's dinner table with his parents, aunts, and uncles. But not once in all these years had he invited a woman along for the ride. His family, he knew, could be a little much for some.

However, during Sunday brunch, Robin seemed to fit in perfectly. That fact alone should have scared him but, somehow, it didn't. Instead, he found himself watching her closely, watching how his family reacted and acted around her.

Everyone was at ease. Even the damn dog wouldn't leave her side the entire time they were there.

Neither of them mentioned to his family that Robin would be moving in with him. It wasn't that they tried to keep it from anyone. It just didn't come up.

"Do you mind if we swing by my place? I need to grab a few more things," Robin asked as they left.

"Sure." He glanced at her. "If we keep whittling away

at it, you should be all moved in by the time the house is done in Hidden Cove," he joked.

She chuckled. "I'm meeting with Blake tomorrow."

"Blake? Why?" He turned into town.

"She's going to let me know what it would take to turn the cottage into a hospitality suite or a rental, depending on the situation."

"That's great," he said as he passed his offices. When he glanced over and saw his business front, he slammed on the brakes. "What the..." He threw the car into park and in a moment was standing in front of his office, looking at his shattered windows.

"What happened?" Robin asked, coming up beside him.

"Not sure," he said as he moved closer.

"You better not touch anything. I'll call Aiden." She pulled out her phone.

He saw it then, the large red bricks that had been thrown through the front glass. Three of them that he could see from out on the sidewalk. It didn't appear as if anyone had actually climbed inside, since there were just several gaping holes and large shards of glass still blocking anyone's entrance.

Two minutes later, Aiden's patrol car parked behind George's car.

"That son of a..." Aiden shook his head. "Larry got out on bail first thing this morning," he said as he stopped next to him. "I'll have him brought in for questioning and restitution. I'll head inside and make sure nothing else is damaged. Got the keys?"

George handed over his key ring. "I'll call Parker and

see if he has a few pieces of plywood to cover the windows until Mia can schedule to get new glass in."

Aiden nodded and disappeared inside.

"I'm so sorry this happened to you," Robin said after he'd gotten off the phone.

He shrugged. "It's just glass," he said as Aiden came back out.

"Good news is that it doesn't appear he went inside. The bad news is, he busted up the back door as well. It appears he started there and when he couldn't get inside that way, came out front and tossed the bricks. He must have gotten spooked and left after shattering the glass."

"Parker's on his way now with a few guys to seal this up," he told Aiden.

"They're looking for Larry now," Aiden said. "I'll keep you posted when we find him. Until then, will you be staying at your place?"

"Yeah, we were just grabbing a few things and then heading over there," George agreed. "We'll stick around here, lend Parker a hand, then head home."

Aiden's eyes moved past him to Robin, who was on the phone with her sister.

"I'll give you a call." He handed him a copy of the police report Aiden had been filling out while they talked. "For your insurance."

"Thanks." George tucked the paper in his jacket pocket.

"Evening," Aiden said to Robin as he passed her.

"Well?" Robin asked him. "Have they caught Larry?"

"Not yet." He wrapped an arm around her. "I'm

going to take you to your place and come back to lend Parker a hand cleaning all this mess up."

"I can help," she started.

He smiled. "As much as I think you'd look really hot sweeping up glass in that pretty dress, I think we've got it. Besides, this will give you time to pack up a little more of your stuff." He pulled her into his arms and kissed her.

She smiled. "I can walk home from here." She nodded. "It looks like Parker is here."

He glanced over his shoulder and saw Parker's truck parking where Aiden's patrol car had just been.

"Are you sure?" he asked. "I can drive you."

"It's only a block away," she assured him.

He thought about what had happened to her sister a few months back. How, less than a hundred feet from where they stood, a mad man had driven by and shot her, twice.

Could Larry be that crazed? He couldn't take that chance.

"I'll drive you," he said again, rubbing her arms. She'd seen him glance over to where Kara had been shot and sighed.

"Okay," she said when she turned back to him.

"Let me just tell Parker," he said.

After dropping her off at the cottage, he spent almost a full hour cleaning up the glass and helping Parker and one of his workers replace all three front windows with large pieces of plywood. Then he helped replace the back door with a new steel security door Parker had on hand.

"You should talk to Josh about putting in a security system," Parker suggested.

"It's on my list to do first thing Monday. I never would have thought that I'd get a busted nose and a busted-up business because of one client."

"From what I hear, Larry Butcher has been trouble most of his life." He sighed. "Rumor has it that he was close friends with Josh's father."

"Brian Williams." George sighed, when he remembered that it was looking like the man would make parole next month. "Yeah, they ran in the same circles. I didn't put two and two together when Laura came in wanting to file for divorce. All I noticed was a scared woman wanting to start over."

Parker lightly slapped him on the shoulder. "Well, for what it's worth, I know that your cousin is thrilled that you're home for good."

He smiled. "Sara's been begging me to come back ever since Ethan and Ellie came along." He thought of his cousin's twins and his smile grew.

"Speaking of which." Parker glanced at his watch and winced. "I'd better get back. It's movie night."

"Thanks, again." George shook the man's hand.

"Sure thing. When the glass comes in, we'll be back to install it," Parker told him before he left.

After making sure everything was locked up again, he drove the half of a block to the cottage.

He really liked the little place with its beachfront charm. But facts were facts. It was tiny. Eight hundred square feet tiny.

He also liked getting Robin further away from her work, since she tended to focus on her job day and night.

Since she'd been staying at his place, she seemed to be growing more relaxed, to be more herself.

Instead of knocking on the door, he let himself in and found her sitting in the middle of a pile of shoes in her bedroom.

"Ready?" he asked, leaning against the doorframe. She'd changed out of the dress into an old pair of jeans and a sweater.

"Why do I have so many pairs of shoes?" she asked him.

He chuckled. "I know better than to answer that question." Then he held up a hand. "Oh wait, I remember what I'm supposed to say. Because no one pair of shoes can contain such beauty." He replayed what his father always told his mother and sister when they asked rhetorical female questions.

Robin glanced up at him and then laughed. "Brown noser." She pointed a shoe at him. "Come help me. I have to narrow these down to a dozen."

"Why?" He moved further into the room. The fact was, he would rather be sweeping up glass and hoisting a large piece of plywood over his head than trying to help any woman decide what shoes she should keep.

"Because there's not enough room for all of these." She motioned to the pile.

"Sure there is." He frowned down at the mess. "The closet is big enough for all of these."

She glanced up at him and shrugged. "These might fit, but nothing else. I have all of that"—she motioned to her massive walk-in closet— "to shove into the closet at your place."

"Okay," he said slowly. "It looks like it will all fit."

"No, it doesn't. Your closet doesn't have the shelves. It only has two long racks to hang things on. This one has shoe shelves, sweater shelves, not to mention—"

He held up his hand to stop her.

"So, we'll get whatever you need. I'm sure Parker would love to get his hands on the closet and make it whatever you need."

"I can't ask him to do that. Not when you're only going to be living there for a few months." She glanced back down at the pile of shoes.

"*We're* going to be living there," he corrected. "Then, in the new house, we'll have whatever you need built in that new closet for a seamless transition."

She looked up at him, her eyes a little wide.

"You... you're really wanting me to move in with you into your new home as well?" she asked, a little softer.

He walked over, took the shoes from her lap, then pulled her up until they looked eye to eye.

"I had hoped," he answered finally. "We can have Parker install whatever you need in the closets, both now and at the new place." He kissed her. "Now, let's clean up this mess, and go home."

CHAPTER NINETEEN

The last days of winter finally gave way to spring. George had been correct—she'd been moving so slowly getting all of her things over to his place, it would probably take three more months to get it all over there. By then, it would only be a few short weeks until she'd have to move it all again into the new house.

Her sister and Conner were planning on moving into their new home, which would be three houses down from theirs, in under a week.

She'd walked through Kara and Conner's place several times with her sister. It had four bedrooms, three and a half baths, and an unfinished basement. It was a different model than the one George had picked out. George's floor plan was the largest one that Rose had designed, with five bedrooms, four bathrooms, and a finished basement.

George's lot was slightly higher up on the hill, and they had, on more than one occasion, watched the sunset from the unfinished home.

She could just imagine how wonderful it would be to live in such a massive, beautiful place.

Her childhood home in Portland had been about the same size but had only had a view of the neighbor's backyard, not the Pacific Ocean.

Her meeting with Blake had gone better than expected. The woman had so many ideas for turning the cottage into a hospitality suite or rental.

Once Robin had all of her and Kara's remaining things out, and once she'd saved up enough money, she was going to start transforming the small place.

Blake had even suggested expanding the front porch so that guests could host smaller dinner parties outside, facing the water.

Blake was working on a graphic that would show her and Kara exactly what she intended to do with the cottage. Robin couldn't wait to see the plans.

The following days after George's office windows had been broken out, the entire town of Pride was abuzz about it. The only strange thing was that the police had yet to find Larry or charge him.

Everyone knew it was the man. After all, Larry had been released less than an hour before she and George had found the mess at his office.

Since that day, George hadn't let her walk or be anywhere alone. Every time she mentioned she was going to go somewhere, he dropped everything to tag along.

She knew why. One would only have to see how Conner was around Kara to understand.

Even though her sister's left arm was no longer in a cast or splint, it was still a lot thinner than her right arm since she didn't use it as much as she had before it had been shot.

Robin knew that there was still a lot of muscle damage that Kara was dealing with, but her mother assured her and everyone that, with time, Kara would have full range of motion again.

She couldn't imagine that the man who had punched George in the bakery would come after her, but she knew that he wouldn't take that chance. Besides, with him around her all of the time, she could keep an eye on him as well.

Once again, it was Sunday, and she was surrounded by Jordans. This time every member of the large family filled the pizzeria in celebration of Todd Jordan's birthday.

Even though the man was turning fifty, he could easily pass for someone in his late thirties or early forties. The fact that all of the Jordan men appeared young, healthy, and just as sexy as George didn't go unnoticed by anyone. Well, maybe not as sexy, but still just as in shape.

No wonder they were a hot commodity. She kept glancing over to George and reminding herself that it wasn't a dream.

The entire pizzeria had been shut down for the private surprise party. Decorations hung everywhere and a massive table was filled with wrapped gifts.

She'd never been to a surprise birthday party before. It was strange, she would have thought that once over the years that she would have, but this was her first.

Just seeing how excited everyone had been to jump out and scream at Todd had made her laugh.

She'd been lucky to have been raised in a loving family, much like George and everyone else there had.

The family laughed, joked, and gossiped as well as cooed over all the younger kids that were present.

Lilly and Riley, who were now extremely pregnant and due any minute, were tucked in a back booth and waited on hand and foot by their husbands, Corey and Carter, and everyone else.

There was a buffet-style pizza bar with every kind of pizza and pasta available.

After the initial celebration, everyone shuffled through the line and settled down to eat.

She and George sat at a table with her sister and Conner near the front of the pizzeria and in the middle of all the mayhem with the younger kids sitting close by.

After most of them ate, things seemed to quiet down some. Then the cake was brought out and everyone started singing.

Everyone had just finished the song and was cheering as Todd blew out all of the candles on his beautiful designer cake when the front glass of the pizzeria shattered. A spray of bullets echoed in the dining room over the screams of everyone trapped inside.

She was tackled to the ground and hit her hip on the ground with a thud. She was quickly covered with a strong body as people around her cried out while they took cover.

Her ears rang when more than a dozen bullets rapidly riddled the area where more than thirty people, thirty family members, including three children under the age of five, had gathered to celebrate.

Her ears rang and her elbows, hip, and ribs ached where she'd been thrown to the ground. George continued to cover her body with his own and held onto her. While lying on the ground, her eyes scanned the prone bodies, looking for her sister, scanning for those three sweet babies she'd just been playing with.

When the shooting finally stopped, several people shouted to block the doors, to get everyone in the safety of the back room. She was pulled up, shoved towards the kitchen area, and crowded into a freezer, then locked in as she lost sight of George.

She only realized her sister was standing safely beside her when Kara wrapped her arms around her and cried.

"He was shot," she kept saying.

"Conner?" Robin's head was swimming, as if she'd just woken up from a deep sleep.

"No." Kara shook her head. "George. He had blood on his arms. I think." Kara closed her eyes and swayed. "I think Todd and Lacey were shot as well."

That snapped Robin out of the daze. Glancing around, she realized Lilly, Riley, and all three babies were safely locked in the massive walk-in freezer with them.

Then she noticed that not a single man was in there with all the other guests.

"What the..." She pushed her way towards the door and banged on it. She was not going to let a gunman kill every Jordan man. This was not how George was going to leave her. Not like this.

"Aiden's on his way," someone said. "The cops will be here soon."

They all seemed to hold their breath then, as they listened for more bullets outside the thick doors.

She shivered, more from shock than the cold, as the thought of George being shot ran over in her head.

How had it come to this? How could this have happened? Why?

"Oh!" Everyone turned suddenly as Lilly cried out, breaking the silence. "My water just broke." She held her massive belly. "No." She shook her head as tears rolled down her face. "Not like this." She glanced towards Riley. "Not when my parents might be..." She bit her lip.

It was then that Robin noticed that several of the women locked in with her had blood on their own clothes.

The entire ordeal was straight out of a horror movie.

"Is anyone shot?" she asked the group.

"No," several people answered back.

"I think I was cut by the glass," Megan answered, holding up her left hand, which was covered in blood. Her daughter rushed over and wrapped a baby blanket around her hand.

"I think we're all okay, just cuts and scrapes," someone said.

Robin turned and banged on the door again.

"George, open this door." She gasped when the door swung open quickly and Carter and Corey stood there, looking a little shocked.

"The police are here now. It's safe..." Carter started to say.

"Corey Brian Miller, my water just broke," Lilly called out.

Robin was pushed aside as Corey raced to his wife. Without pausing, she rushed from the freezer to find George.

She passed Aaron as he worked on Todd, who was lying on the floor, eyes closed, blood pouring from his chest, his shirt covered in blood. Megan had followed her out and ran to her husband's side, crying as she knelt beside him while their son Matthew helped Aaron.

Glancing around, she found George near the front of the pizzeria. He was holding a clean towel to his mother's thigh, his own clothes covered in blood.

Seeing that he was healthy enough to help his mother, she hurried to him. Their eyes met and a silent message passed between them.

Lacey was sitting in the booth, her right leg propped up on a chair as George held a towel to her thigh. Kneeling beside him, she placed her hands over his and helped apply pressure to his mother's leg.

"I'm okay," Lacey was saying as she took George's hand. "I think it was just glass that cut me when your father threw me to the floor and covered me."

"George," Robin said as she glanced up at him. "You're bleeding."

He glanced down at his bloody arm and nodded. He showed her a large gash that crossed his forearm. The wound didn't look too bad. Still, she guessed it would need a few stitches. Then he wrapped the towel around it again. "Something grazed my forearm. It's just a graze," he assured her after placing his hand over hers.

"Go, help the others." She motioned towards his

family. "I've got your mother." She motioned. "Oh, your sister's water broke in the freezer."

Lacey's eyes widened as fear flooded them even more. "My grandbaby."

"Is fine. Lilly looked fine," she assured them both. Robin watched as tears filled and then rolled from the woman's eyes as she looked for her daughter. George disappeared into the crowd.

"Corey's got her. Let's worry about you right now," she told Lacey.

Robin hadn't noticed any police in the area yet, but now, two officers walked in. She'd met both of them before, several times. Simon, an older man, moved over and started talking to Aaron while Tom, a man just a little older than she was, stood just inside the doorway, looking a little pale and sick as he scanned the carnage.

She glanced around the room, assessing the rest of the family.

So far, Todd appeared to be hit the worst. Several other people were bloody, but everyone else was up and walking around or, in Riley's case, sitting.

Lilly was being half carried, half dragged towards the door by George and Corey now.

"Leave me alone," she was practically yelling and crying at the same time. "I'll wait until they take Uncle Todd first."

Kara came to sit next to her. "How are you feeling, Mayor?" she asked Lacey.

"Like I want to find whoever did this and..."

Just then Aiden walked in. He hadn't been in attendance at the party, and Robin had overheard Suzie mention that he would be showing up to the party after his shift ended.

Now, as he walked in, questions were shouted at him as EMTs rushed in behind him.

Aiden held up his hand after taking Suzie in his arms and kissing her.

"I've got the shooter in custody," he shouted over the questions. Everyone quieted down except Aaron, who was relaying Todd's vitals to the EMTs.

Everyone watched and waited in silence until Todd was rolled out on a gurney. Aaron assured them that he would take very good care of his brother-in-law and see everyone at the hospital, then he followed them out.

Lilly let out a soft squeal as a contraction almost doubled her over.

"No!" She shook her head when her husband and George tried again to pull her towards the door. "I'll go after I hear Aiden."

"I had just gotten off shift and was less than a block away when I heard the shots. I rushed here and found Kevin Williams reloading an AR-15. He's sitting, cuffed and bloody, in the back of my patrol car now."

"Kevin?" Allison asked, then turned to Iian and signed. "I thought he was locked up."

"He got out on parole two days ago," George said, his eyes turning to his mother.

Lacey sighed. "I thought it was best that only a handful of people know. After all, there was no proof that he was going to return to Pride." Robin's eyes moved to the cop standing still just inside the doorway, his eyes still huge and filled with fear. "Josh, Tom, and Brenda all filed a restraining order against him. He wasn't supposed to come back here." Lacey shook her head and closed her eyes.

"How in the hell did he get a gun?" someone asked.

"I'm going to make it my mission to find out. Whoever gave him access to it is going to be held responsible," Aiden said as he hugged Suzie again. Then Aiden walked over towards Tom.

Tom Williams, Kevin Williams' oldest son, stood dressed in his dark blue police uniform. When Aiden touched his shoulder, he folded down into a chair and covered his face.

As she watched, Allison moved over and wrapped her arms around the man's shoulders and said something softly in his ear. Then a few other family members joined her until he was surrounded by love.

Aiden glanced around. "Who else is injured?"

Robin watched as more EMTs came in. They rolled Lilly out next, then she moved aside as they came and took Lacey.

Moments later, she walked outside with George and noticed that there were close to a hundred townspeople standing around, watching.

When each person walked out of the pizzeria, the crowd clapped and called out cheers and praises that they were okay.

"Sir." An EMT stopped George. "I'll need to check that arm."

"We're heading to the hospital now. I'll have it checked there," George replied.

The man looked like he wanted to argue, but she stepped in.

"I'm driving us and will make sure he gets it looked at immediately," she told the man.

"Let me at least wrap it for the trip," the man offered.

George looked at her, and she nodded quickly.

She'd already arranged to drive Kara and Conner as well and they all waited as George's arm was quickly cleaned and wrapped.

When the four of them piled into George's car, she felt her entire body start to shake. She didn't even realize she was sitting there, taking several deep breaths, without even starting the car. Then George was pulling her into his arms and holding onto her.

"We're okay. We're all okay," he said into her hair. "My uncle's in surgery now. My dad says he's got a good chance." He sighed heavily. "He's strong."

"It's his birthday," she said quickly. "He was shot on his birthday."

CHAPTER TWENTY

George sat in the waiting room of the hospital in Edgeview, along with the rest of his blood-covered and bruised family members and waited in silence.

Almost every single one of them had bandages covering cuts. To a passerby, they would appear to have been a large group of partygoers who had ended up in a brawl instead of a shooting.

Everyone kept saying how lucky they'd been. That it could have been much worse. He knew they were all just consoling each other while they waited for word of Todd's outcome.

Shortly before midnight, Corey came down to the waiting room, full of smiles.

"Benjamin Todd Miller was born at eleven thirty-three. He weighs seven pounds, eight ounces and is a glorious twenty-one inches long," he said happily. At some point he'd changed out of his blood-soaked clothes and into clean scrubs.

The silence was replaced with happy cheers and

congratulations as Corey passed around his phone to show the chubby-cheeked, bright-eyed baby.

Since his mother had disappeared up to the maternity ward shortly after being stitched up, he knew that she'd been by his sister's side the entire time.

He wanted to go see the new baby but wanted to wait until he wasn't covered in blood and sweat.

He told Corey to tell his sister that he'd see them in the morning. Corey hugged him and agreed, then told him that Lilly and baby Ben were resting comfortably.

"I'm also sending your mom back down to you. She's tired and worried about her brother."

"I'll come wheel her down myself," he suggested.

"No need." Then he handed George his phone. "Now, look at your nephew," Corey said with a smile.

"He looks like me," George said with a grin as he looked at the photo of his sister looking tired but happy as she held a very small baby that had the Jordan eyes, chin, and mouth. He could see a lot of Corey and Carter in there as well. Pride had tears stinging his eyes.

Robin laughed. "All babies look alike."

He gasped and shook his head. "You have obviously not seen enough Jordan babies. Each one is perfect."

She hugged him. "Congratulations, Uncle George."

Less than half an hour later, his dad walked into the waiting area, dressed in scrubs and smiling. "Todd has made it through surgery just fine. He's resting now and can start receiving visitors in the morning. Megan, you can go back and see him now. He's awake and asking for you." He nodded to the nurse, who showed his crying aunt through the double doors. "Now, I'm going to go see my new grandson and then take my wife home. I suggest you all do the same."

His dad walked over and wrapped his arms around his mother, whose leg had been bandaged after receiving close to a dozen stitches. She also had a pair of crutches to use while she healed. She'd been wheeled to and from the maternity ward earlier, since there were plenty of wheelchairs available to her.

Then his dad walked over and hugged him for the longest time. "I love you, son," he said before turning and wheeling his mother towards the elevators.

George's arm had needed six stiches across the forearm where he'd been told a bullet had grazed him. He'd expected it to be a piece of glass, like his mother's leg, but the doctor who stitched him up said it was definitely a bullet wound.

The entire family exited the hospital quietly like a bunch of dazed zombies.

While Conner drove the four of them back to Pride, he held onto Robin in the back seat of the car.

"We got lucky today," Conner said softly.

"Yeah," they all agreed.

"You knew that Kevin had gotten out of prison?" Conner asked him.

"Josh asked me to look into his potential release a few weeks back," he told them. "I knew there was a possibility, and I found out he'd made parole a few days ago. We did everything we could to keep him from coming back to Pride." He leaned his head back and took a deep breath. "I should have—"

"Leave it," Conner broke in. "There is no way you

could have known. Just like Brenda, Tom, Suzie Williams, or even Josh couldn't have known what he would do. We're just lucky Aiden was there and caught him before he could reload and enter the pizzeria."

"You locked us in a freezer," Kara reminded him.

Conner reached over for Kara's hand. "We didn't know if he was going to storm in and keep shooting."

"So you strong-armed us into a freezer?" Robin asked, glancing over at him.

"We just wanted to protect what's ours," George said.

"And what about you?" Robin asked. "Why weren't you in there with us?"

"You too," Kara asked Conner.

Instead of answering, George pulled Robin closer and kissed her.

"Okay, that's one way to shut us up, but too bad you have to keep your hands and mind on the road," Kara poked Conner on the shoulder. "So, tell me what your excuse is."

"It was just..."—he shrugged— "a gut reaction."

"We didn't really think," George added as he looked into Robin's eyes. "I just wanted to protect the woman I love."

"Aww," Kara said softly.

"Shush." Robin waved her sister's mocking tone away. "You... love me?" she asked him.

He smiled. "If after what we just went through today, I can't say it freely... I doubt there's any better time to say it. Yeah." He nodded and sighed as his heart did a little flutter. "God, you're so beautiful."

"Don't change the subject." Robin pushed his chest.

He smiled. "Can this wait until we're alone?" He nodded to the front seat. "And after I've had a shower and some sleep?"

"Pretend we're not here," Kara said quickly.

"Unless you start to get freaky back there," Conner said, earning him another slap on the shoulder from Kara.

"Want to ride together in the morning?" Conner asked as they pulled up to their place so they could drop them off.

"Sure. I'll want to see if Suzie can arrange to have some flowers ready for both Lilly and Uncle Todd."

"Good idea." Conner nodded. "I'll send her a text. Maybe she can have something ready for us in the morning. We'll pick you up, maybe swing by the bakery for something sweet and some coffee before we hit the flower shop?"

"Sounds good." They all got out and changed places, with Robin driving now since she refused to let him drive with his arm hurting.

George took a moment to hug his cousin, then hugged Kara as well. "Night," he said and climbed into the passenger seat.

"Well?" Robin said after a moment of silence as she drove them home.

"My god." He relaxed back and closed his eyes. "Do you know, I used to love gangster movies. You know, the kind where the gunman stands outside the Italian restaurant and shoots everything up." He glanced sideways at her, his heart and head hurting as flashes of what had happened earlier played in his head. "I don't think I can ever watch one of them again. Not after..."

His voice cracked and she reached over to take his hand in hers.

"I know what you mean," she said softly. "It was nothing like the movies." He felt her shiver, the vibration moving through her arms.

"I'm sorry," he said suddenly.

"For?" She glanced over at him.

"I don't really know. I mean…" He sighed as he closed his eyes and rested his head back as she parked in front of their place. "If I had told my family that Kevin was out, that he was…"

"Don't be a fool," Robin said as she shut off the car. "There is no way you could have known the man would do something like that. I mean, my first thought was Larry."

"I know, me too." He sat up a little. "You can bet I'm going to make sure that man has no way to get to us now. I mean, threats from all sides." He shook his head. "Maybe I shouldn't have come home?"

"Don't say that." She took his hand, and he noticed her eyes running over his fresh bandages. "Don't let them win. Let's go inside, finish off the left-over cherry pie we have in the fridge, take a shower together, and then fall asleep holding one another, knowing we're both safe. That everyone we love is safe."

He smiled a little. He knew he had to shut it all down and get some sleep. He'd think through his next steps in the morning when his brain was working again.

Later, however, as he lay listening to Robin's soft breathing as she lay wrapped around him, he ran through what he wanted his future to look like. How he could better his life for him and his family.

In the end, as he fell asleep, the one steady thing that rang true was that, whatever happened, his family's love was the strongest force in his life.

The following morning, when they shuffled into the waiting area with the rest of his family, he smiled at all the flowers and balloons and all of the well-wishers from Pride.

The entire hospital waiting room was filled by noon. His uncle had been moved to a private room, and he'd had a few moments to visit him with some of the rest of his family.

Todd looked better than he'd expected and was sitting up in the hospital bed, surrounded by flowers and his immediate family. There was a large bandage over his right shoulder and his right arm was tucked tight against him with bandages.

"How are you feeling?" he'd asked him after shaking his left hand.

"Alive," Todd said with a smile. "It's not how I expected my birthday party to end," he joked lightly. He sighed. "We got lucky."

"Yeah." How many times had he heard that over the past few hours? The truth was, they had.

"Kevin Williams has always had it out for us. He's been sending letters to Allison for years. Our lawyer..." Todd sighed. "Our ex-lawyer, since I plan on officially switching everything over to you when I'm up and about, had been receiving them for years. Allison used to teach Tommy and

Suzie Williams and was instrumental in getting Kevin a longer sentence after his DUI, since he'd admitted to her that he'd burned Ally's mother's house down after attacking and knocking her out." George remembered hearing the story. He hadn't, however, remembered that his aunt had taught Tom and Suzie. "I hear you knew that he'd gotten out?"

"Yeah." He felt the guilt hit him again. "His family had me get restraining orders against him. The man wasn't supposed to step foot in Pride, let alone get access to a weapon. It was part of his early release terms."

"Yeah." Todd motioned to his son-in-law, Aiden.

"The weapon was registered to his brother, Carl. We're looking for the man now," Aiden informed him.

"Carl?" he asked. "I've been trying to locate the man myself."

"If you find him, let us know," Aiden added.

"Will do."

From there, he and Robin spent some time with his sister and baby Benji, as he was calling his new nephew.

Holding the little boy, he couldn't help but imagine what his own children would look like one day. The fact that his mind kept combining his and Robin's features together had his smile growing.

From there, the four of them stopped off and ate lunch at a seafood restaurant in town before heading back to Pride.

It was as if the entire town of Pride had stopped. Just seeing the windows of Baked bordered up, much like his own business had been a few weeks back, had his temper growing.

Since it was Monday, he figured that he'd head into

the office and see if he could use his anger as fuel to hunt down Carl Williams himself. Leaving Robin to catch up on her rest, he headed into the office.

"What are you doing in here?" Mia asked the moment he walked in his office door.

"This is my business," he reminded her.

She smiled and rushed around the desk to hug him. "Go home, be with your family. I'm just rearranging your appointments."

"That's fine. I wanted to spend some time on a more... personal mater anyway." He smiled down at the older woman. "Pretend I'm not here." He headed down the hallway to his office.

An hour later, his eyes were blurry, and his head was aching. Still, he followed the trail that Carl Williams had taken when he'd left Pride.

George remembered Josh mentioning that Carl had moved to California with his mother after she and Kevin and Carl's father had divorced.

When he finally tracked down the woman several hours later, he realized why it had taken him so long to find her. Lisa Carson-Williams had changed her and Carl's last names to her maiden name. A short search later, his entire body vibrated with anger when he stared at a grainy picture of the woman and her son, Kevin Williams' younger brother, Thomas Carl Carson.

CHAPTER TWENTY-ONE

Monday night's event was large, but by no means the largest she'd hosted. After a very long nap to catch up on her sleep from the crazy day and night before, Robin headed over to the barn and was actually looking forward to a little normalcy.

She knew that George had gone into his office before she'd laid down and as she headed into work herself, she'd sent him a text message telling him that she'd be home around eight. He'd replied that he'd meet her at the cottage instead.

Both Kara and Emma rushed around to get everything ready for the children's birthday party.

Tonight's venue called for cowboys, horses, and everything boy. She'd set up several fun events such as calf roping, which included kids roping a bale of hay with horns on it, a bucking bronco ride, a cowboy hat toss, and a bushel bucket beanbag bonanza, as Kara was calling it.

She had to admit, it was just what she needed to lighten her mood.

After all, everyone was safe. Everyone was alive. The bad guy hadn't won.

"We should do this more often," Kara said, sitting down in the chair next to hers.

She smiled as the last of the guests left out the front doors. "It warmed my heart seeing all the kids have fun," she agreed. "I've decided that we're going to leave the cleaning for the morning." She put her feet up on the chair opposite her. "I've already sent everyone home for the night."

"Yes!" Kara did a quick fist pump. "I heard you got to see the new Jordan man." Kara wiggled her eyebrows.

"He's technically a Miller man," she said and then giggled at her own joke. "Benjamin Todd Miller." She sighed. "I love that they named him after his great-uncle. After all, he was born on his birthday." Robin's smile slipped slightly. "George tells me he's doing well. He's expected to head home in a few days."

"Being shot takes a lot out of you," Kara said as she rubbed her left arm. "I was lucky. Todd..." She shook her head. "I just remember seeing all that blood coming from his chest. There was so much more of it than when I was hit."

"I know." She reached over and took her sister's hand. "This small town has been extremely lucky of late."

"Yes." Kara sighed. "Well, now that the party's wrapped up, and I don't have to stick around and help you clean, I'm going to head home and get some rest," her sister said, covering a yawn.

"I'm right behind you. I wanted to grab a few things from the cottage. I'm trying to take a box every time I'm here. George is going to meet me there." She glanced down at her watch. "In ten minutes."

They made sure the place was locked up and then hugged before Robin walked over to the cottage.

She'd packed up most of her things, since Blake wanted to start on the remodel that next weekend. The only items remaining in the cottage were the things she didn't necessarily want to keep. She'd thought about doing a garage sale but had decided to donate them instead. She only had three boxes left of her personal items and figured they could take the rest of it home that night.

She heard George's car drive up and park and had started to carry out the boxes when she smelled the smoke. Seeing the dark cloud come from the back of the barn, she dropped the box she'd been holding and rushed towards the growing fire.

"Robin!" George grabbed her arm moments before she rushed into the opened back door.

"It's burning," she cried out clawing at George's arms. "I have to stop it."

"You can't stop it," a deep voice came from behind them. "Everyone in this town needs to pay for what they've done to my family. To my brother." Carl Carson stepped out of the darkness; a gun pointed directly at them.

George pushed Robin behind him quickly, shielding her once again.

She could feel the heat of the flames behind her, but her focus moved from losing her business to losing the man she loved.

"Why?" George asked. "Why burn the barn down?" He nudged Robin back a foot.

"It's there," Carl said with a crazed smile. "I tried to play nice with your family. I really did." His voice raised. "I used all my skill, all my money, all my power to try and burn this town to the ground. Everything must burn!" he yelled, spit spewing from his mouth, and Robin watched in horror as the gun shook in the man's hand. "It must disappear. It's been nothing but a black mark on my family. It's caused my brother to be locked up, my nieces and nephews to go against me. Even my own mother hates it and everyone who lives here. They turned their backs on us long ago." He stopped and then smiled. "The barn is the biggest, oldest structure. It's close enough to town that the fire will spread, taking everything with it. I hadn't expected you two to still be around, but..." He shrugged slightly and took a step closer to them. "I've cleaned up my mistakes before." He raised the gun.

"What mistakes?" George asked. Robin wanted to run, to yank George away and just... run. But instead, he stood there, blocking the madman from her and talking to him like a... well, a lawyer. "What mistakes have you cleaned up?"

"The idiot I hired to do the job in the first place, Kurt Collins." He laughed. "It was easy enough to nudge his truck off the road after he botched the simple task of getting you out of the way." He motioned to Robin. "Course the man couldn't tell the difference between you and your sister." He rolled his eyes. "And that stupid Herold Jenkins started talking after starting a side project gambling ring. I'd hired him to blackmail, not raise his own funds. When he came begging for legal help, well, I had to make him disappear." The man seemed to have gotten lost in his story, but now shook his head clear and refocused on them.

Robin could hear the crackling of her business, of her life, being destroyed behind them. Still, her focus was solely on the gun pointed at George's chest.

"Even Larry." He laughed. "Poor stupid Larry. I went to school with the man, along with Joe Nelson, both idiots." He shook his head. "Joe was easy enough to buy off, so he'd log in and delete some files, then go around and shut businesses down. Too bad he got caught." He shook his head. "Had to get rid of him. Couldn't leave a paper trail, you know. Then Larry came to me after he got out on bond when he'd punched you." He motioned to George. "He begged for help to pay his legal bills and help in fighting his divorce. He even tried to blackmail me into helping him." He laughed. "Worst mistake ever." He smiled suddenly. "So when my brother finally got out of jail and came to me a few days ago, I nudged him in the right direction. After all, he was primed to get payback on your family. Supplying him with the weapons was easy enough. He proved stupid as well, since he was supposed to wait until after I burned the town down, but I'm sure seeing all of you Jordans in one place, well, he couldn't pass up on the opportunity to take his revenge." The man's face changed. "It's too bad he didn't take a few of you down in the process. Although I hear he got Todd square in the chest." He laughed. "That man was always an arrogant ass. Went to school with him too. I bet you didn't know that his first wife, Sara, and I used to be an item." Carl smiled. "She was the love of my life. Then Todd waltzed in and stole her from me." He spat the last part out. "I should have killed him years ago."

"Why didn't you?" George asked.

It was then that Robin knew George was stalling. She could hear movement behind her, the faint sound of feet rushing towards them just reaching her ears over the crackle of the fire consuming the barn behind her.

"I figured the only way to beat him was to outpower him." Carl shrugged. "I went to school, started my own business, became a millionaire, only to have him take it all away again," he shouted.

"How did he do that?" Robin asked.

Carl's eyes snapped to her. "I spent millions persuading investors to back my resort plan. I was going to steal this town right out from under his nose. Then when Todd came in and purchased the land out from under me, my investors took off with all my money, and the board of my own company voted me out. Took everything that I'd worked so hard to build. I was left scraping the bottom of the barrel to try and hold it together." He shook his head. "I lost everything because of him. Because of this fucking town! Because of your fucking family. Every single Jordan has to pay."

"Freeze!" Several shouts echoed as bright lights zoned in on Carl.

Once again, she was shoved to the ground. She watched in horror as the man raised his gun towards the lights and fired, just before several bullets tore through him, sending him flying back into the darkness.

This time, thankfully, the soft sand and dirt had cushioned her. She turned to look up into George's eyes.

"Are you okay?" George asked her immediately.

"Yes. You?"

"Yes," he sighed.

Her eyes traveled to where Aiden was checking on the man who had caused so much harm, killed so many others. Then her gaze moved to where the red glow and smoke continued coming from the kitchen area of her business.

"I called Aiden before heading over here. I figured we'd just talk and that I'd fill him in on what I'd found out. But then I noticed a strange car parked at the end of the block and called him again before I pulled in here. I found out that Carl is Kevin's brother. Thomas Carl Carson-Williams." He sighed.

They could hear the fire trucks as George helped her up off the ground.

"It's ruined," she said, wiping tears from her eyes as the fire crew got to work putting out the fire.

"What's going on? We heard the fire trucks." Kara and Conner came rushing up to hug her. "How did this..." Kara's eyes moved past them to where Aiden was covering Carl's body.

"My god, are you guys okay?" Conner asked.

"Yeah," George said, wrapping his arm around Robin as they watched the firemen work.

Kara hugged her as the men tried to save their business, everything they'd worked hard over the last year to build.

By the time the fire was out, half of the town had

come out into the night to see what was going on. The story of what had happened spread just as quickly as the fire had.

She was sitting on the front porch of the cottage along with her parents and a few of the Jordans when Lane Auston, chief of the fire department, walked up. He'd removed his helmet but still had on the rest of his gear.

"Well, you ladies are extremely lucky. When you had Parker revamp the kitchen, he installed a state-of-the-art fire prevention system that kept the fire localized and from spreading into the older part of the structure."

"It's safe?" Robin asked, feeling a sense of relief wash over her.

"It is. You'll need to do some major cleanup, since he sprayed the back door with fuel. It was a good thing he couldn't get into the property. We all thought the entire place was going to go. It appears the back wall, inside and out, got most of the damage." Lane shook his head. "We all owe Parker thanks. If this place had gone up." He shook his head. "It would have taken a few more firemen and firetrucks to stop it from spreading," he said before he turned and walked away.

"That's what he had planned," Robin said softly. "I'm going to have Parker install the new fire system in the entire barn when he does all the repairs."

He smiled down at her. "That's a great idea."

They filled Aiden in on everything Carter had confessed to. How he'd gotten rid of both Joe Nelson, whom they hadn't known was missing, and Larry, whom they still hadn't found. Aiden assured them that they would find both men and that hopefully, they were still alive. But they both doubted it.

"I guess I'll need to reschedule all my events," Robin said after Aiden had left.

"Honey, if it's just the kitchen, maybe Joy and the staff can use the kitchen in here since you're not staying here," her mother suggested. "I know it's smaller, but if the rest of the barn isn't damaged..."

"Tomorrow. For now, shut it down. We'll get in there in the daylight and assess the damage," George said. "Then plan how we're going to work around the mess." His arm tightened around her.

"Agreed," Kara said. "Let's go home," she said to Conner as they both stood up.

George's parents had been standing next to her own parents for most of the past hour. The four of them left shortly after her sister and Conner had.

Once everyone was gone and they were left alone, George pulled her into his arms.

"Let's go home," he said into her hair. "Shower, since we smell like smoke, and once again, try to turn everything off."

"I don't think I can." She shook her head as she closed her eyes. When she saw the image of her business burning, she opened them again. "How about a walk?" She nodded towards the beach.

"I can go for a walk," he said, taking her hand.

It was one of the first really warm nights of the year, and she knew that there would be a lot more to come in the following days.

They walked along the dark beach. The soothing sound of the waves somehow settled her further.

"We need a dog," George said suddenly.

She stopped, turned, and looked up into his face. The soft moonlight caused his eyes to almost glow.

She hadn't expected the tears, but when his arms wrapped around her, they flowed freely for the first time that evening.

"Or a cat. Oh god. Don't you like dogs?" he asked. She laughed and wrapped her arms around him.

"I love dogs," she cried into his chest.

"It's okay. We're okay," he assured her while she cried.

She pulled back a few steps. "I don't want to be okay." She took a deep breath. "I don't know if it's possible to try and be, after all this."

He leaned back slightly with a look on his face as if he'd been punched in the gut.

Walking towards him she wrapped her arms around him again. "Not us. This has nothing to do with us."

"But it does." He held her back so he could look her in the eyes. "And you're right. We can do better than just okay." He shocked her slightly by dropping down on his knee. "I was starting to plan some big grandiose gesture, but..." He kissed her knuckles. "If you can forgive the last minute of this, I promise to spend a lifetime making it up to you." He smiled up at her and she felt her eyes sting once more. "Robin, I know we started out together both just expecting to enjoy a roll in the hay." She chuckled. "Then things changed. We changed. You changed me. You've made me better, made me wish for better for myself. I can't imagine not being there for you. Not having you by my side during trying times. I hadn't expected to do this, but I fell in love with you." He brushed his lips across her knuckles again.

"I love you too." She smiled, feeling her heart jump in her chest again. Only this time it was a good feeling.

"Marry me," he said, meeting her eyes. "Please. I can't stand the thought of going a day without you. Please say you'll marry me."

She smiled and bent down to kneel in front of him. Taking his face in her hands, she kissed him. She poured everything she felt for him into the kiss.

"Is that a yes?" he asked between kisses.

"Yes." She smiled. "I think you can take me home now."

He pulled her up, wrapped his arms around her, and held on long enough that she felt the rest of the stress from the past few days dissipate.

Less than a week later, George sat beside Robin, surrounded by family once more. Only this time, everyone crowded into his Uncle Iian and Aunt Allison's place, the Jordan's original home. The one his great-great-grandfather had built when he and his wife had settled in Pride all those years ago.

There was plenty of food, laughter, and love as everyone watched Todd, who sat propped up on the sofa, slowly open his birthday presents.

George doubted that anything could ever take the man down for long. Even being shot in the chest. Technically, he'd been shot in the shoulder, but according to his father, the bullet had come within inches of vital organs.

He laughed and clapped along with the rest of his family members while holding onto Robin tightly. They had yet to tell his family of their engagement and had decided to wait until after Todd had opened all of his gifts.

Riley had gone into labor two days after his sister had given birth to Benji and sat across from him holding little Aurora Lane Miller. The two new mothers and fathers beamed with pride when anyone came near. He had to admit, the kids were some of the best-looking babies he'd ever seen.

He and Robin had talked, while lying in bed, wrapped around one another, about children. They'd both agreed to having three. It was the perfect number. Three kids and three dogs.

He knew she and Kara had been relieved to find out that the damage hadn't spread into the main part of the barn. The kitchen and Robin's office, however, had been destroyed. Not enough that it couldn't be repaired, but enough that it was blocked off until Parker could get to work.

Joy had assured them that she and the crew could work out of the cottage, just as long as she could plan the meals out ahead of time since it would take them longer to cook in the smaller kitchen.

For now, Robin had moved her office back to the cottage while Blake started remodeling the rest of the place and getting it ready to rent out.

It was determined that Thomas Carl Carson-Williams was responsible for four murders after Aiden had found both Joe Nelson's and Larry Butcher's bodies in the trunk of his car.

His brother, Kevin Williams, was going to rot in a jail cell for the shooting at the pizzeria.

He and the rest of his family finally felt like the immediate threat was over.

As far as George could tell, he had everything he ever wanted. His eyes ran over his and Robin's joined hands. There was nothing like the feeling of having someone to love, someone who he knew he would love for the rest of his life.

The Pride Series

Finding Pride

Discovering Pride

Returning Pride

Lasting Pride

Serving Pride

Red Hot Christmas

My Sweet Valentine

Return To Me

Rescue Me

A Pride Christmas

The Secret Series

Secret Seduction

Secret Pleasure

Secret Guardian

Secret Passions

Secret Identity

Secret Sauce

The West Series

Loving Lauren

Taming Alex

Holding Haley

Missy's Moment

Breaking Travis

Roping Ryan

Wild Bride

Corey's Catch

Tessa's Turn

Saving Trace

The Grayton Series

Last Resort

Someday Beach

Rip Current

In Too Deep

Swept Away

High Tide

Lucky Series

Unlucky In Love

Sweet Resolve

Best of Luck

A Little Luck

Christmas Wish

Silver Cove Series

Silver Lining

French Kiss

Happy Accident

Hidden Charm

A Silver Cove Christmas

Sweet Surrender

Second Chances

Entangled Series – Paranormal Romance

The Awakening

The Beckoning

The Ascension

The Presence

The Calling

The Chosen

Haven, Montana Series

Closer to You

Never Let Go

Holding On

Coming Home

The Hard Way

Pride Oregon Series

A Dash of Love

My Kind of Love

Season of Love

Tis the Season

Dare to Love

Where I Belong

Because of Love

A Thing Called Love

First Comes Love

Someone to Love

Wildflowers Series

Summer Nights

Summer Heat

Summer Secrets

Summer Fling

Summer's End

Summer's Wish

Distracted Series

Wake Me

Tame Me

Stand Alone Books

Twisted Rock

Hope Harbor

Raven Falls

For a complete list of books:

http://JillSanders.com

ABOUT THE AUTHOR

Jill Sanders is a New York Times, USA Today, and international bestselling author of Sweet Contemporary Romance, Romantic Suspense, Western Romance, and Paranormal Romance novels. With over 70 books in eleven series, translations into several different languages, and audiobooks there's plenty to choose from. Look for Jill's bestselling stories wherever romance books are sold or visit her at jillsanders.com

Jill comes from a large family with six siblings, including an identical twin. She was raised in the Pacific Northwest and later relocated to Colorado for college and a successful IT career before discovering her talent for writing sweet and sexy page-turners. After Colorado, she decided to move south, living in Texas and now making her home along the Emerald Coast of Florida. You will find that the settings of several of her series are inspired by her time spent living in these areas. She has two sons and off-set the testosterone in her house by adopting three furry little ladies that provide her company while she's locked in her writing cave. She enjoys heading to the beach, hiking, swimming, wine-tasting, and pickleball with her husband, and of course writing. If you have read any of her books, you may also notice that there is a love of food, especially sweets! She has been blamed for a few added pounds by her assistant, editor, and fans... donuts or pie anyone?

Join Jill's Newsletter and get book and sales updates monthly. https://jillsanders.com/newsletter.html

Remember, if you've enjoyed this book, please leave a review where you downloaded it. Thanks

facebook.com/JillSandersBooks

twitter.com/JillMSanders

amazon.com/Jill-Sanders/e/B009M2NFD6?tag=jillm-com-20

bookbub.com/authors/jill-sanders

instagram.com/jillsandersauthor